My first Novel
a little bit of me &
mine .

Happy New Year .

Love

Chris

X

D1743176

The Seven Paperweights

Christina Godley

authorHOUSE®

AuthorHouse™
1663 Liberty Drive
Bloomington, IN 47403
www.authorhouse.com
Phone: 1-800-839-8640

© 2013 by Christina Godley. All rights reserved.

No part of this book may be reproduced, stored in a retrieval system, or transmitted by any means without the written permission of the author.

This is a work of fiction. All of the characters, names, incidents, organizations, and dialogue in this novel are either the products of the author's imagination or are used fictitiously.

Published by AuthorHouse   03/26/2013

ISBN: 978-1-4817-8896-0 (sc)
ISBN: 978-1-4817-8897-7 (e)

Any people depicted in stock imagery provided by Thinkstock are models, and such images are being used for illustrative purposes only.
Certain stock imagery © Thinkstock.

This book is printed on acid-free paper.

Because of the dynamic nature of the Internet, any web addresses or links contained in this book may have changed since publication and may no longer be valid. The views expressed in this work are solely those of the author and do not necessarily reflect the views of the publisher, and the publisher hereby disclaims any responsibility for them.

Great Balls Of Fire.

25th December, 1986.

The luxurious warmth of a half awake Sunday morning feeling became suddenly chilled by the loud hammering on the front door.

'WAKING UP LUFF! TITS AND BUMS ALL OVER GARDEN! BE QUICKING COMING DOWN!'

Eve stretched and yawned, then cursed her Polish neighbour for disturbing an erotic dream involving Robert Redford, a log cabin and a tub of chocolate ice cream. Her thoughts flooded back in grainy images, then reality kicked in and she groaned.

'ALL right! I'm coming. Hold on!' she shouted, grabbing her dressing gown and running into the empty back bedroom. Below her, Anton Morawski, was chasing wildly round the garden, trying to catch the remains of last night's bonfire.

Her Soon-to-be-ex-husband had left her for a younger, slimmer woman who thrashed him at tennis and happened to be a cookery teacher! She could cope with the younger, slimmer and sportier bit, but a good cook as well was hard to swallow. During the process he'd stripped the house of all furniture while she was at work, leaving her with: the spare-room single bed, an old black and white television, the broken recliner and his crazy cat: Heathcliffe.

The husband's habit of flopping down into the chair in a huffy sort of way, brought about its demise, owing to his 6'2" body with size 12 feet. Now the green velvet heirloom, left by his vindictive old Grandmother, had two positions: a tricky, deceiving upright and a total flat-out recline. Many an unsuspecting visitor had been caught unawares in the comfy looking trap.

In the end Heathcliffe became "Lord of the Springs," until

the husband removed every other seating arrangement in the house. Then it was a constant battle between her and the frantic feline. Through trial and error she discovered that if she sat very still, the chair would remain in the upright position - and it was better than sitting on the floor, until the mad cat came indoors.

Despite all this, she had developed an attachment to the old chair, as it was the only constant fixture in her life. The only advantage of having so few possessions was that she didn't have much to pack up for the imminent move on 2nd January. The "Sold" sign outside creaked in the biting wind, reminding her that she would be homeless in the New Year.

'Hurrying up luff! There being many bums in "Bobby Wooman's" garden. It's good job she be staying with sister-in-law until New Year!'

Right at that moment she had a strong desire to throttle her lovable friend. Her frustration, as always, soon subsided when she helped him catch the fluttering disembodied pieces. It was a mystery though, why those fragments that hadn't burned were the ones bearing four letter words and erogenous zones.

Last night, as her birthday drew to a miserable close, she had made a wine-warmed tottering ascension up to the loft to check its contents. Dirty finger-prints on the hatch-door gave away the fact that he had also rifled all of the good stuff up there. While ignoring the old wooden bedstead and obviously forgetting about his stash of girlie magazines in the carrier bags behind the water tank. He was preoccupied with thoughts of the forceful four-course dinner and "Miss Whiplash" awaiting him at his new abode. When Eve discovered the contents of the carrier bags she didn't know whether to laugh or cry. It was her forty second birthday for God's sake! According to Douglas Adams: "Life the Universe and Everything = 42." Momentarily seeing the irony of this discovery, she threw the heavy bags, one by one, down onto the landing. Then swearing like a Lottery Winner who has lost a million pound ticket and found a fifty pence down the back of the sofa, she finished with a flourish, shouting: 'Tosser!'

Although it was nearly eleven o'clock she decided to have one last purge and took a hatchet to the remains of the old bedstead, which had already broken into pieces on its ejection from the loft.

The bonfire flickered warmly in the darkness, then turned into a blaze as she poured on some lighter fuel. She slung the offending magazines into the flames, not noticing the woolly-hatted head peering over the fence.

'Wanting some help luff?' Anton asked kindly.

'Yes please!' she replied, startled by his sudden appearance. Realizing that she must have scared him too, looking like a demented Banshee. Her red hair escaped from its gripped constrictions, frizzled crazily around her face. Not used to alcohol, her cheeks and neck also turned a glowing shade of crimson.

After she explained to Anton about the magazines he started to chuckle. 'It being a buggering up luff. You should be giving them to his fancy wooman!' he laughed. Eve adored the old widower. He was the most honest person she had ever known. His personality was one of passionate extremes. He loved his late wife Maudie, Heathcliffe because "he killing rat" and Eve. But he hated the Germans and the "Bobby Wooman" next door. So here they were singing a belated "Happy Birthday" and dancing round the bonfire like a pagan witch with her side-kick Rumplestiltskin.

Long after Eve and Anton had gone to their beds the magazines slowly burned into the night. From the singed curling edges to the shiny centre-folds, the exposed pages smoldered on through to Christmas Day.

Now in the cold light of morning, like giggling children, they had managed to confiscate most of the explicit bits to a bin-liner. Then Anton cleared the "Bobby Wooman's" garden, which ironically, had attracted all of the raunchy parts. A huge pair of purple tipped nipples hung on the bare branches of the apple tree. Anton chuckled at the thought of old Ma Winters finding these fruity offerings on her pristine land. She would definitely have called the Police - and the Fire Brigade.

After the embers died away she went inside to make a warming drink. The cupboards were almost empty. Since the husband had abandoned her, she needed far less food. No longer did she have to spend half her salary every month, at the Supermarket. Him piling in luxury items and her daft enough to pay for them. She remembered how he had eaten twenty choc-ices in one evening, without so much as leaving a sliver for her. And that he had taken the fridge/freezer the day after she'd filled it.

Sipping her hot chocolate she watched Heathcliffe in the recliner, pondering how to prize him out with the battered tennis racket. Having second thoughts when he growled and spat at her. All notions of tiredness and her bleak future suddenly dissolved, as a loud hammering on the front door shattered her thoughts. Two pubescent broken voices murdered the first verse of "Silent Night."

It was a family tradition never to turn the first carol singers away, or something untoward would ensue. She felt some relief when they didn't attempt the second verse. The only change she had was a pound coin and, reluctantly, handed this over. One of the spotty youths grabbed the money and said in a cracking voice: 'Ta! Missus! Merry Christmas,' before inflicting the same punishment on the next house. They rang the bell for about five minutes before realizing there was no one home.

A loud rattling on the door startled her again. This time they'd not even bothered to sing. She was just about to tell them to "Push off!" until she recognized the familiar outline through the glass window. Anton's twinkling blue eyes peered from under his woolly hat.

He stood on the door step in front of her like one of Santa's little elves. Behind him was a wheelbarrow containing: two deck-chairs, picnic tables, a steaming cooked turkey with all the trimmings, a bottle of red wine and a half bottle of cloudy Polish vodka, plastic tumblers, a box of Christmas crackers - and a boneless kipper for Heathcliffe.

After dinner they tried to lure the crazy cat from the recliner with a piece of kipper attached to the tennis racket, but the cat always won claws down. So instead the two friends settled back in the deck-chairs with a shot of vodka each and watched "It's a Wonderful Life" on the old black and white television.

'It's a good job it not being a colour film luff!' Anton chuckled.

It's All Over Now Baby Blue

26th December.

'Hello! It's only me!' Eve's older sister Angela phoned tell her that they were just about to set off to spend Christmas in Florence with her only son Richard. Her two daughters preferred the excitement of the big city, enjoying a Designer shopping Christmas with friends in London. Also they couldn't stand their parents constant bickering. 'Our Meg and Geoff are coming with us. Aren't they Keithy?'

No "Happy Birthday" then? What about "Merry Christmas?" Or even "How are you?" she thought. Greetings Earthling? Kiss my arse? She sighed, knowing Angela just wanted to talk about herself.

Eve continued to eat her porridge, with the phone locked between shoulder and ear. Although she could quite easily have finished off a full English breakfast without uttering a word, and her sister wouldn't have noticed the difference. Stretching out the kinks in the telephone cable, she reached up to the kitchen cupboard and took out the honey pot, while Angela talked about all the Christmas presents she had received from her husband. A hug blob of golden sweetness trickled into the porridge. That's better, she thought as she returned to the stool and continued to eat.

Her eldest sister, Meg hadn't mentioned much about the holiday, but then she wouldn't want to hurt her feelings.

'Keith bought me a lovely diamond ring-. How many carats is it Keithy?' Keith muttered something. 'It's three quarters of a carat. Aren't I a lucky girl?'

On the few occasions Angela phoned either of her sisters, it was always to brag. She wondered how much overtime Keith had worked to pay for it. She usually switched off and listened, making the right noises in between. But owing to a recent revelation she felt sorry for her sister and had more patience than usual.

'Do you want to speak to Keith?' Angela asked, in her baby voice.

'All right then,' she replied, hating the thought of talking to the man who was betraying her sister.

'ALL right then,' her sister's mocked in a drawling voice, as Keith took the phone from her.

'Happy Christmas Sweet,' he said.

'Likewise Keith and the same to Tracey as well!' Eve bit her lip but she had to say something. Tell her brother-in-law that she knew about his affair.

'Err! Righto then Evie. All the best.'

He quickly passed the phone back to Angela who twittered on for another hour about herself.

'Everyone said that my Christmas Dinner was the most delicious they'd ever tasted. And our Kirsty said that I was the best cook in the world and should take it up professionally,' Angela twittered on.

Dinner lady, thought Eve.

'My mince pies melt in the mouth. Don't they Keithy?'

Put one in your mouth now to stop yourself talking shite.

'Our Sarah said that my Christmas cake was better than Marks & Spencers.'

Give me a chunk so I can stick it in my ears.

'Anyway. I'm going now...We're having cocktails from our new cocktail shaker...All right then,' before hanging up.

And goodbye to you too.

Eve could hear her father's voice somewhere in the back of her head saying, "Our Angela could talk a glass eye to sleep." Her sister was one of those people who could chatter for hours and never say anything memorable. She was always friendly, but absolutely unaware of anyone else's need to talk. Believing that her lack of information from the other person, was because they had nothing to say. Not that they couldn't get a word in edgeways. It never dawned on her that a conversation was a two-way street, with pauses in between to allow the other person to have their say.

Angela was always the main protagonist in her own dramatic elaboration, whereas Eve and Meg became introspective when upset.

They just clammed up, not wanting to burden folks. Angela was one of those women unable to acknowledge others' feelings, or show any form of sympathy to those worse off than herself. To compensate for this lack of understanding, she frequently portrayed herself as the nicest sister to anyone would listen. That way she could spread herself around thinly among people she hardly knew - and at the same time malign her unsuspecting sisters. She had pushed too many friends and relatives away from her because of this superficial bravado - and her massive ego.

Eve thanked God for her zany friends at the Council. Shirl and Mavis in particular were her favourites. Despite being sorely abused by their ex-husbands, their apparent optimism astounded her. Mavis would say: 'When I'm eighty there'll still be a ninety year old man who fancies me.' And Shirl knew she would get his mate. They loved a gossip and would hang on to Eve's every word, then add a few of their own to make the story more juicy. The two wacky divorcees who constantly wanted to talk about their sex lives and hers. After which they would retell everyone else her innermost confessions. Until her intimate problems became the public property of whoever needed a bit of scandal. Someone else's issues helped them forget their own. Chinese whispers gathered momentum. The two women relayed and embellished them through the grapevine at tea-break. When everyone had discussed the infamous goings-on and had a laugh, the tasty morsels became trampled underfoot with the biscuits crumbs. Then they were forgotten.

Strong coffee! she thought, stretching out her arms above her head and rubbing her neck. Sitting in one position for too long had aggravated her back problem. She opened a tin of Whiskas with chicken for the mad cat, mashing it up into a paste, as the aging feline had only one remaining incisor. He ignored it and wailed for something else. Something else being the left over turkey. She cut some slices into small pieces, dropping them onto the cat food, and he ate the lot. Angela had talked her through the morning up to what now was lunch-time. The Polish vodka was lethal and her head was pounding like the battle-speed drums in "Ben Hur." She stuck out her tongue and groaned, then took two Aspirins.

She knew her eldest sister Meg wouldn't tell Angela anything about the divorce. Because, in Angela's case a problem shared was a problem doubled. Your distress would become her heartache and her heartache would be your fault. These days Eve did everything possible to avoid burdening her sister, as she always seemed to be on the edge of her own tragedy.

Angela hadn't always acted so spitefully. The rot set in after the family's first holiday in Skegness when the cracks appeared in the otherwise perfect child. She was eight years old and Eve was nearly four. Although only a toddler, she remembered the events clearly, as it was the first and last time she'd seen her father really angry. What she remembered most about that particular holiday, was her mother's mouth swelling up like a frog's from sun-burn, a plague of ladybirds settling on a woman in a yellow jumper - and Angela getting a slap from her father. He'd never struck any of his daughters up to and beyond this moment. "The pen is mightier that the sword," he would quote.

They had arrived singing merrily: "Ten green bottles..." in Cedric Netttleship's "Shooting Brake." An estate car with wooden panels. To this day she didn't know why the car had this name. As a child she always thought it was because the brakes used to shoot out bullets. When they saw the sign: "Welcome to Skegness" with a picture of a jolly fat sailor on it, they knew they'd arrived. Their father told them to lick their first fingers and stick them out of the windows. 'If you lick your finger again, like this, you can taste the sea,' he knowingly informed them.

Her sister was always a friendly child and chatted to anyone within shouting distance. After the first week the happy holiday mood turned to one of gloominess for the whole family. Eve could still hear her mother's hysterical crying behind the bedroom door of the guest house. The happy holiday mood came crashing down around their heads. Eve was shut out on the landing with Meg and could only hear their father's voice getting louder and louder.

Angela gave as good as she got, shouting back at her father. There was a hard slapping sound, an intake of breath, then Angela's heartbroken sobs, followed by her screams resonating through the door, as she bawled out: 'I hate you!' Eve remembered being frightened for her sister and tried to get into the bedroom, but Meg held her back.

Her sister had wandered off that day as they relaxed on the beach. She was missing for two hours, after being found in the Gents toilet, crying her eyes out. She told everyone that she'd walked in there by mistake and that she'd got scared. And that a woman heard her sobbing and took her to the "Lost Children's Hut," where, according to Angela she sang and danced, making everyone laugh. It was true that Angela had the voice of an angel, so her father eventually believed her, wanting it to be true. And that was the end of the matter.

It was only two years ago on Eve's fortieth birthday, Angela confessed to what really happened. The real story was that a man found her on the beach and led her away on the pretext of looking for her parents. She trusted him until he forced her down the stone steps and locked the toilet door behind them. She knew that something was terribly wrong. He told her to be quiet or he would suffocate her. She still believed he only wanted her to use the toilet, until he unzipped his fly.

Angela had broken off telling her story at this point and couldn't continue for a while. Digging her nails into the palms of her hands and trying the erase the image in her mind. She began to shake, remembering that dreadful event from her childhood. So afraid, unable to tell in case people believed her to be wicked. After all those years of suffering in silence, she finally confided in Eve, hoping it would make her feel better.

Hoping it would somehow go away. It didn't. All she felt was anger and shame. The foul smells of urine, the bottle green paint on the walls, the passing shadows above and the sound of clattering feet on the opaque glass tiles in the pavement. These things closed in on her and remained in her memory for the rest of her life.

Eve remembered her sister talking in her little girl's voice as she told her story. Her beautiful eyes sad and puzzled. Eve held her sister and cried with her. She suggested counseling. Yet as soon as Angela finished her story, Eve realized her sister had regretted it. She acted as if the terrible secret she held onto all those years, was now lost forever; beyond her control. She trusted Eve implicitly, but felt worse for the sharing. So in her mind she conveniently forget about their conversation, transferring her latent anger onto her younger sister. It made life easier.

From then on, the only way she could communicate with Eve, was over the phone. That way she didn't have to see the pity in her sister's eyes. The child's confusion became the woman's guilt. The fear never left her. Despite reassurances from Eve, she still believed she was bad and that she would probably go to hell. The two sisters never mentioned the incident again.

☙

Eve looked into the near empty kitchen cupboard, fancying something sweet. There were two tins of Green Giant corn, a box of Oxos, a packet of pasta shaped like Christmas trees, a packet of Carr's water biscuits and a tin of lychees. She thought that every kitchen cupboard in the country must have a dusty tin of lychees lurking in its nether regions. She'd never met anyone who liked the fruit and wondered why, in a fun packed Christmas Bumper Hamper, there was always a tin of said fruit. A tin of cling peaches would have been a better option. At her parents house there were always cling peaches for Sunday tea, and Carnation milk, along with jelly and custard. Meg updated the pudding menu when she discovered blancmange. A creation of whipped up melted strawberry jelly with Carnation milk, left to set in the trifle bowl on the pantry slab. A tin of John West Red salmon for starters with a chunk of Cos lettuce, a tomato and lashings of salad cream. With thick slices of bread and butter to fill their hungry mouths. A feast spread out on the best white linen table cloth.

After a round of turkey sandwiches, followed by two of Mr. Kipling's exceedingly good Bakewell tarts covered in leftover custard, Eve looked lovingly at the recliner. Heathcliffe was curled up into a ball and farting silently in his troubled sleep. She decided to take her tea up to the bedroom and sort out the knickers-drawer instead. The empty house echoed even the smallest of sounds. As she walked up the stairs she noticed the square patterned carpet. Mitch had chosen it and she'd never liked the design. It was shabby now, like the wood-chip wallpaper on the landing. She'd intended to have the carpets professionally cleaned before the move. The stink of cat pee won hands down over the air fresheners and disinfectants, so she did a daily "Shake'n Vac," to cover the odour.

She'd tried locking out the mad cat at night, but he wailed constantly. She even provided him with a lit-tray, cat-nip toys, and feline well-being hormone spray. He still preferred the carpet. The worse half of the purchasers, Pauline Jackson and her constant demands, swayed Eve to change her mind. Let Moaning Minnie sort it out, she thought. The outdated white tiles in the bathroom and the strip light-fitting had seen better days. The box bedroom with the tiny single bed, with shelves full of soft toys. Now her nighttime abode, although Heathcliffe thought it his.

Inside the main bedroom the badly fitted wardrobes with doors that didn't close, were filled with clothes two sizes too small. She now realized that she would never be a size 10 again. It didn't matter anymore. Making a mental note for her New Year's resolution, she decided to stop buying big cardigans, to join a gym - and be happy with a comfortable size 14. Quickly she bundled the size 10 clothes into carrier bags and threw them down the stairs.

The top drawer was full of lacy things she hadn't worn for ages. The comfortable white sports bras and briefs lay neatly pressed on top. Underneath the tangle of silky bras, pants and tights was a small brown box. Painful memories flooded back. The box contained: a half knitted matinee coat, a tiny flannelette nightgown and a soft baby brush and comb. It felt like a lifetime ago, when Mitch brought her suitcase to her parent's house. For some reason he'd packed all the pants he could find but forgot to bring any clean clothes.

Love Me Do.

She had pushed this awful time some twenty five years ago, out of her thoughts. Now the dreadful reminder twisted like a fist in her stomach. The old aches mingled with the new. She was seventeen and a half years old and couldn't wait to tell him the news. It was their first wedding anniversary and he'd forgotten the date.

Girls like herself married young because it was the expected norm in the village. Only three types of women lived in the narrow-minded community: the married lady, the tart and the old maid. She didn't want to be any of these. Her sisters were born before the War and glided into the first accepted state with ease. Even the rebellious Angela did everything the same as Meg, only with more panache. Her sisters were all flounces and flares in aiming for the hour glass shape, with circular-stitched pointed bras, suspenders, and pantie-girdles, whereas the Sixties had created a waif-like gamine look, with panda eyes, pale lips, tights and visible knicker-lines.

Momentarily she felt again a sense of wonder at being a Teenager in that era, and far away from the limbo-land in which she now found herself. There had been a new kind of freedom that had arrived in an explosion of colour. For the first time the young had choices, espresso, thigh boots - and like David Bowie, believed there might be life on Mars. Crazy days when each new experience was "Fab" and "Groovy" and every hour an adventure. The fashions changed weekly, each becoming more outrageous than the last. Whereas during the Fifties when the majority of children left school at fifteen years of age, they were expected to instantly become adults. Ankle socks swapped for high heels in one swift movement. Now in this new exciting age, as Teenagers, they could stay young and act foolishly. At least they thought so at the time.

Youngsters could give up their jobs on Friday and start a new one on Monday. People in the know and considered to be intellectuals, like David Frost and Bernard Levin, ended their important words with -ism. Satire was reborn and inhibitions were thrown into the wind of starched shirt flaps. A place full of new sounds and sights, that made her forget the constant thud of the factory lump hammer pounding through the night. The pylons too near the house - buzzing and crackling in anger. And filthy rain puddles that splashed the backs of her legs, leaving greasy black marks.

In the extraordinary time of change there was the promise of a whole new era. Post War shortage was filled in with: Bob Dylan, The Rolling Stones, Mary Quant miniskirts, Cleopatra eyeliner and abstract thought. Girls actually danced on their own in the dance halls, and didn't have to trip the light fantastic backwards on high heels. All the "wall-flowers" were liberated from the edge of life. They took to their feet and danced round their handbags - hoping. Feminism had arrived and the world was a brighter place.

Her sisters had none of this "new fangled rigmarole" and became irritated when she mentioned D.H. Lawrence or Betrand Russell. Their natural order threatened by what appeared to be anarchy. They only read "Woman's Weekly," the same as their mother. The married lady's only new item of clothing was a smaller pinafore with frills on. 'Always got her nose in a book, trying to be different,' Angela would say, as if it was some sort of weird thing to do. When really, she was only trying to find herself. It was the only way to find out different things regarding the outside world. In the end even her mother succumbed to wearing tights and a mini skirt.

On reflection she realized the Sixties had by-passed Blackridge, wafting over the top with the smoke. Second hand images and sounds, via the television and radio, filtered through the smog. No first hand experiences ever savoured. They had to travel to Sheffield and The Locarno for the real immediate sensations. They didn't do this too often as the lads there were more aggressive and really fast. They were called "fly," by the village girls and were to be avoided at all costs.

Nevertheless, she, Vee and Peter, had definitely felt the Sixties in their hearts and minds. They imagined the local dance hall was "The Cavern," and the amazing raw sound of: "Love love me do," was sung live by the Beatles, not a record on a gramophone. The nearest she got to her fifteen minutes of fame was getting Cliff Richard's autograph. Their family doctor was at a party and he got the singer to sign a bit of paper. It said: "To Eve. Best Wishes. Cliff Richard." Elvis never did reply to her three fan letters.

Eve and her friends, finger-daubed "Ban the Bomb" logos in the dust of factory windows and on the few cars parked outside. Their praises echoed around the valley to Betrand Russell, albeit not really understanding his philosophy. Once they saw a red "Zephyr Zodiac," belonging to the gaffer's son, and they were so amazed by it's uniqueness and colour, they tried to rub some of the dust away with their hankies. Angela caught them in the act and told their mother. Eve got into big trouble for "vandalamism" - one of her mother's malapropisms. "I blame that "Vanilla" Redgrave!" she had said.

On her wedding day, four months after her sixteenth birthday, Eve saw her youth slipping away. It was as if she was being forced under the lump hammer at the Steel Works, and having the life squashed out of her. She was pushed into a loveless marriage and be a "nice" girl, just to fit in with the rest of the community. They were to live with Mitch's Gran, renting her sitting room. The old woman was so miserable it was said: "Her face would fall in half if she laughed."

There was no excited chatter, before her wedding, only a still hush and a few crushed carnations. At her sisters' weddings there had been such laughter and jollity. Her wedding guests seemed as downhearted as the Bride and Groom. Her dreams of a princess wedding dress, were replaced by a cream jacket and skirt, with chocolate brown accessories, because Mitch didn't like any fuss. He considered honeymoons a waste of money. Any form of showiness, or emotion frightened him. Stan had intended to hire the Co-op Hall, but Mitch insisted on Eve making sandwiches and trifles on her wedding morning at Old Gran's house.

She had so wanted her mother to bring her breakfast in bed, as she had done for her other two daughters on their wedding day. She desperately needed to hear her father say how lovely she looked. Instead she had dressed herself in Old Gran's second best bedroom and came downstairs to two sullen faces. The only comment she received was from Mitch, who said resignedly: 'We'd best be off then and get it over with!'

The Registry Office was even worse. Everyone looked uncomfortable, not used to civic proceedings. A wedding without a vicar, prayers, or hymns was, in their eyes, invalid. Even jolly Auntie Blanche looked puzzled at the mismatched pair. The stammering unsmiling Registrar peered at the couple over his spectacles and read out the words in such a pompous way that Angela burst out laughing. In a state of enforced optimism, Eve wanted to believe when Mitch said: "I do," her life would change for the better. Inside she felt sick and isolated.

He stood by her side with arms folded, and stiff backed as if he had a poker up his arse. Wearing the same old suit that was two sizes too small, with trousers at half-mast. Not once looking at her, as he echoed the words, without emotion or meaning. Uncle Billy whispered to Aunt Iris, shaking his head: 'They'll be tears before bedtime.' No hymns were sung, no prayers uttered. Only a crowd of relatives shuffled out of the Town Hall feeling uncomfortable. As the confetti fluttered around in the wind, she hoped he didn't feel the same desolation.

O My Beloved Father.

Her happiest memories were those of the visits to the Allotment with her father. They sustained her. Despite the suffocating feelings associated with her birth place, the village never left her. Sometimes she would smell the dust from the factories, or hear the pounding of the great hammer that used to rock her to sleep every night. The images and sounds were fleeting but reassuring. It was as if the village had been caught in a time warp in her mind. It's funny, she thought, how the things we most want to get away from as children, become the idealized stuff of dreams upon reflection.

Nothing edible grew in Blackridge. Stan attempted a vegetable patch but the black polluted soil, clumped together with clay, was reluctant to yield a crop. Every garden had briar roses and lawns littered with dandelions and buttercups instead. One time he had actually grown some Savoy cabbages, but the day they were ready for cutting they were stolen by a couple of cheeky youths from the old village. Stan decided there and then that he would never again attempt to plant vegetables in his back garden. Instead a privet hedge covered the concrete posts and wire. He grassed the whole area and planted leggy pink roses and lavender in the borders. Fortunately he had kept up the rent on his father's Allotment, on the higher ground. This small plot of land was his domain, a place where he felt most at ease.

On sunny summer weekends, when he didn't have to work over-time at the factory, he would sit her in the wheelbarrow and start the long walk up to Waterwell and on to Brambleton. Through the Broom and Hawthorne hedges neatly trimmed, and past the Engine Pond, where he had ice-skated as a boy. Now hundreds of tiny frogs hopped around, fighting to get back into the water as the wheelbarrow rolled by. The farms and the smell of pig-manure and cow pats made them both wrinkle their noses. Onwards up the steep hill and past the church, where he always bought them an ice-cream each from Kettlebrough's farm shop. It tasted like heaven, fresh and creamy, full of goodness and needed to be eaten quickly before it melted.

When they arrived at the plot, her father immediately started hoeing, weeding and digging. There was always work to be done. A flower or vegetable for every season. She watched him cover the seeds with the dark rich soil, then tie out a lattice-work of brown string, to keep off the birds. She would help, until she got bored. Then she would sneak off to her favourite place round the back of the greenhouse. A patch of land where the wild strawberry grew, where she would eat her fill, cradled in a semi-circle of sky blue hydrangea bushes marking the boundary, and next to the greenhouse full of tomato plants heavy with fruit.

There was a shed holding gardening tools. Inside it was full of interesting things for little fingers to explore. A set on tiny labeled drawers, contained seeds and strange brown beans that were warm to the touch. Underneath the drawers was a shiny hearth plate with red poppies and ivy leaves painted on. And an old left-handed mangle confined to the shed because: "It was no use to man nor beast," her mother had declared. Behind the sheers and rakes hung on nails, was an iron hobbing foot, slowly rusting, and no longer used, with fresh wood sawdust scattered over the floor that smelled of pine.

She watched her father labouring, until his back turned the colour of the earth. Giving her young sweet carrots to sample and approve. Then he would wipe his head with a red hankie and walk over to the water trough. There was always an old man seated there, wanting to talk to the younger man about "hardy annuals" and "grafting." Her father would roll a cigarette. Taking a delicate paper from the packet, he'd sprinkle a line of tobacco, then roll a the cigarette between blackened fingers. Licking the edge to seal it, before giving it to the older man. Then he would repeat the ritual, with a dexterity unusual for such powerful hands.

She loved the smell of strong tobacco, mixed with earth and sun, and the sweet odour of dahlias. While they talked she filled the metal watering can from the moss covered tap. He laughed when she struggled to carry it over to the greenhouse, wetting her sandals. Their sandwiches were eaten and flask emptied. After which the flowers were cut and neatly tied into bunches, for selling in the village. Vegetables consisting of green beans, garden peas, carrots and new potatoes, carefully placed in the wheelbarrow. Tomato filled bags hung on the handles. And at the end of the day he would carefully lift his sleeping daughter and put her amid the day's rich harvest, to start the long journey home.

ɞ

After marrying Mitch she missed those long quiet summer days. Days held in time, that lasted forever. The simple pleasures of her childhood dissolved. Now she expected to be a mother by the time she was eighteen. 'A young mum has got to be a good thing,' she reassured herself. Looking forward to walks in the park with her sisters and their children.

Happy thoughts flooded in about her future life with the baby. Colourful pictures and books around, to brighten the place, making changes for the better. She and Mitch would finally talk about everything without embarrassment. There would be an end to oppressive atmospheres and definitely no secrets. Their lives filled with ideas and imagination. Her baby told how much joy she had brought into her parents lives. Her childlike optimism exhilarated. Without a doubt Eve knew she was having a daughter.

Her mother often told her how disappointed she was when a third girl was born. Rose had so much wanted a boy. She'd even chosen a boy's name: Gary after "Gary" Grant. The stork decided to leave another girl. When the ginger-haired bundle was handed to her on Christmas Eve, she offered it around to any takers. Eve knew her mother didn't mean to hurt her feelings, but as a child she'd felt a savage rejection. She vowed never to harm her child with thoughtless words.

Like the time she asked her mother, under which tree she was born. Her mother had said that Meg loved bananas so much she must have been born under a banana tree. Angela was know as "Apple Angela" because of her rosy cheeks. Eve imagined Angela as a rosy faced baby, gurgling under an apple tree. 'What tree did you find me under Mum?'

Her mother thought for a while, then laughed, saying: 'A gooseberry bush!'

Eve had never seen a gooseberry, until she started school dinners. Usually they had jam roly-poly, or spotted-dick and custard, for pudding.

'Ug! It's goosegob pie,' her classmate Jane complained. 'Disgusting!' When the pudding plopped into her dish, it smelled delicious. Thick custard added on top completed the new taste experience. Only when she returned to the dinner table to try her namesake fruit, did she realize her mother's joke.

'Snot and bogie pie. Snot and bogie pie,' sang Steven Green.

Eve scraped the pastry away from the fruit and saw the vile mixture underneath. After that, only the brave few could eat it. From then on she assured herself that her birth tree was a pomegranate. She'd tasted one once and loved picking out the red jeweled fruits with her Nan's hat pin.

Whereas poor Mitch had been bombarded with rejection. Constantly told by Old Gran he should never have been born and made to feel he was worthless. She called him "the bastard of a worthless twit." If her child had problems they wouldn't be left unresolved. Unfinished sentences hanging in the air. This little one would bring a breath of fresh air into the gloomy household. Soften her cold hearted husband. Give him the incentive to leave the depressing family funeral business. Live in a different atmosphere to that he'd known, where children were unseen and not loved. To be heard in her parents' home was paramount, even if it merited a slap, when their mother could catch them. Three sisters competing for attention and determined to get the better of Rose. And they did - every time.

Here she was at seventeen, living in a household of misery. No laughter heard. Not so much as a curse in anger broke the silence. The three of them resided there in disharmony, Mitch, Old Gran and herself trying to avoid each other. She accepted the friction in her parent's house. The constant disagreements soon ended. They kissed and made up. Everyone in the family talked over each other, vying for front position. Her aunts and uncles visited by the dozen. Each one of them loud and noisy, with hearts of gold and little loyalty to each other.

Nevertheless, what Eve remembered most about that time, was parenting was a difficult task. It meant absolute sacrifice. Her mother and father did everything possible to make their children's lives easier than their own. At the same time they tried to maintain the strict discipline they had known. Ultimately giving their children a strong sense of who they were and where they belonged.

Many children in the Sixties were brought up differently in a post-war world of progressive thinking. Their mothers tried to be their best friends. Named their children: Ziggy, Tarquin, Julius, Freeway, Cyclone, Sky, or worse. They tried to hold on to their youth - and still do, looking like embalmed monkeys in Designer gear. Back then they always dressed garishly bright and trendy, regardless of how ridiculous they looked. Sometimes they wore the same outfits as their children. Even grannies bought miniskirts. Ironically the demarcation lines removed by "The Age of Aquarius" parents only made their off-springs confused over who was the adult.

Once on her way to work she saw a child, rolling around on the floor screaming in temper. His desperate mother tried to reason with him.

'Now then Donovan Aurelius' she said. 'I shall send your presents back to Father Christmas, if you don't stop kicking mummy.' The child continued to scream and kick. 'Please Donovan, tell mummy that you're going to be a good boy, then I'll buy you an ice cream.'

'Disgusting behaviour!' a passing pensioner remarked to Eve. 'Needs a belt taking to him.'

'No,' she replied. 'He just needs to know who is in charge.'

The new generation of pant swingers and cheese cloth singers with tambourines, dreamed of a world without violence and tried to paint the dark-side of humanity with rainbow colours. She had thought the same and dreamed of a new universal order of pacifism. "Bows and bells and angel's hair," against tanks and guns and radiation glare. In reality a no win situation. Sadly, she thought, if some Neanderthal has a big stick, it's necessary to get an even bigger one, or run away. Not sing in his ear about love and peace when he's about to tear off your head.

☙

Eve felt complete with this other life inside her. The tiny human being which dominated her body and gave her cravings for peaches. She waited for Old Gran to go to bed before springing the surprise, nervous but quietly confidant everything was going to be all right. After enjoying the special anniversary dinner, she held his hand and told him about the baby. His response threw her completely off balance.

'What? You idiot! ...Why have you done this to me?' he said, scraping his chair back on the wooden floor.

She heard the floor-boards creak and knew that Old Gran was listening at the door. The frail looking old woman, dressed in black, with her neat silver hair in a bun, had all the finesse of Godzilla. 'Is "it" his?' she asked, barging into the sitting room.

'Course is! I've never been with anyone else,' Eve protested.

'What were you thinking of you pillock!' Old Gran turned on Mitch. 'Anyone would think "rubbers" hadn't been invented...I don't want any pewling babbies in this house. Don't think I've worked my fingers to the bone to support another no good waster. Another mouth that'll want feeding, at my expense no doubt...Both of you! OUT! Do you hear me!'

What the unsuspecting folks didn't know was that the local chemist's mischievous sons were sticking pins in the Durex packets, thereby increasing the Derbyshire population thrice-fold.

'Just leave us Gran. I'll sort it. She knows what's best! Don't you Eve?'

Old Gran shuffled out of the room, grumbling under her breath and unlocked the cellar door. No one knew what was down there, but it certainly wasn't coal. The sound of clattering jars and bottles often heard in the dead of night. It was said that she collected: eye of bat and tongue of toad to flavour her morning porridge. In fact she was a bit of a scientist. Mixing up potions had become a sideline to the funeral business.

Mitch tried to convince his wife how wrong it was to have a baby at this stage in his life. After failing miserably to persuade her, he flopped into Old Gran's new recliner and sulked.

'It might be a boy - and look like you,' she pleaded.

'But it might not.'

She ran to the loo and threw up, tears streaming down her face, then put some things in a bag and tried to leave. He struggled to take the bag from her, his face unmoved and ashen. Freeing herself she wrenched the case out of his hands. She couldn't bear the thought of him touching the few baby clothes she had tenderly packed. Old Gran came up from the cellar carrying a glass of green coloured liquid.

'Now! Now!' she soothed. She reminded Eve of the wolf who had eaten chalk to soften its voice. 'Leave the poor girl alone for a minute! Here Eve lass, drink this. It'll stop you being sick! There's nothing worse than vomiting all the time.' The closeness of the old woman made her feel worse, especially that awful smell of mothballs.

'What's in it?' she asked, her head spinning.

'Just a few herbs and juices. It'll help you relax as well. We'll all feel better after a good night's sleep. Now drink it down all in one go. We'll talk in the morning...There's a good girl.'

The magic words! Eve had always been a good girl for her Mum, Dad, Nan and even now - it still worked. Old Gran pressed the glass to Eve's lips and she gulped the foul tasting liquid back.

Mitch didn't come to bed that night, falling asleep in the recliner. Old Gran crept to bed silently, for a change. Usually before bedding down for the night, she made a terrible fuss about them burning too much electricity, before pouring the teapot dregs onto their fire, saying the same as always: 'I'm going to bed! Don't be long!'

The pains were dull at first and climbing the stairs was a huge effort. Eve looked around their bedroom, as she leaned against the door. The only place where they had any privacy. It looked neat and welcoming with the sky blue curtains. Her parents had bought the matching blue silk eiderdown as a wedding present. Over the bed the soothing picture of Monet's blue water-lilies from Meg. Uncle Billy had framed it with walnut wood. The blue fur teddy pyjama case from Angela, nestled on the bed. On the dressing table she had arranged her seven paperweights on the crotchet mat Auntie Iris made for her. Either side was a blue glass candlestick holding a white candle.

She lit the candles and took out the white towels from the bottom drawer, when the pains worsened. Then she pulled back the sheets, folded the towels and placed them on the mattress. Tossing and turning she woke up pouring with sweat. The wrenching agony in her stomach was more tenacious now, unbelievable searing pains like she had never known - and then the bleeding came. Slowly at first and before long gushing out all over the white towels. Her terrified cries silently ignored. She only hoped her prayer was not.

The next morning Mitch had prepared breakfast for them all. The cooking smell of bacon made her retch. He and Old Gran sat at the kitchen table silently waiting for her. Neither of them gave her any eye contact and she couldn't stand to look at them. She filled the copper boiler with water, pushed the soiled articles down inside, and turned the gas heater on to maximum. Something she'd not dare do before. Without a glance back, she put on her coat and closed the back door.

After two weeks at her parent's house she started to feel a little better, but refused to see her husband. She hadn't told her parents about the baby so her family couldn't understand what was happening.

'Why don't you see the lad. He's really upset,' her mother asked. ' "In sickness and in health," Evie... Look at the lovely flowers he's left you.'

'Funeral white flowers. The musty smell of lilies,' she said. 'The stink of death!'

When she finally came downstairs from her sickbed he was waiting quitely. He told her everything would be all right and they could always try again later. He painted a rosy picture of the future, the house, the children, the holidays, the dog. She almost believed him.

Later on that evening in Old Gran's gloomy sitting room, the place where many a poor soul found it's last resting place before burial, he put his hand on her shoulder and tried to reason it out. 'Look Eve!' he said, pressing her to sit down. 'If I cut my little finger off and at the same time there was an earthquake at the other side of the world, killing thousands, what do you think would be more important to me?'

'What do mean?' she asked.

'What you never know, you'll never miss.'

No seventeen year old should ever experience the hatred and bleakness she felt.

~

Was this what men really thought? Once a rogue spermatozoon had battled its way out of a faulty condom, it no longer had any connection with its origins. Excess bodily fluid sent out into oblivion, like a sneeze or a cough. The ejaculator exonerated from all further responsibility.

Do men want to be fathers only when their children move beyond: sleepless nights, constant feeding, changing, burping, nursing? Or the first stumbling steps and faltering words? Eternal questions? Chicken Pox? Sulks and strops? Adolescent acne? Locking horns? Heart break? Infatuation? Exams and fees? Weddings costs? Mortgages? Babysitting their grand children?

Was it only women who could visualize the future? See the child laughing and playing. Family resemblance noted. Perfectly formed fingers, surprisingly strong, and tiny feet with shell-like nails, examined. Miniature replicas adored. Photographs framed, by the score. Protective of every move and anticipating accidents before they occur. Surely not! Her own father had done all these things to secure his children's well-being.

ↅ

Her life was never the same. All optimism sucked out. Too scared to tell her parents, she carried the guilt around with her like a penance, blaming herself for being so guileless. It would have been too much of a shock to face up to the truth.

Just Like A Woman

She fingered the faded baby clothes and placed them back in the drawer, knowing her chances to have children were slipping away. She cried silently, until there were no more tears left. Can't turn the clock back, she thought, remembering one of her father's sayings. "Life must go on", was another. "Enough is as good as a feast". She wished she had his optimism - and that these bloody adages would take a hike. All she could muster at that point was "Life's a bitch and then you die," echoing the words of the master of bitter irony: Woody Allen.

Drinking her cold tea she slung all the lacy black pants into a carrier bag and mentally thought how well they would rekindled yesterday's bonfire. She hurled the bag down on top of the others and put the comfortable pants back into the drawer. Her hand caught on something sharp, wedged into the corner at the back. A small gold key.

Wiping her eyes, she held the key up for closer inspection. It had a faded piece of ribbon attached. It looked familiar, but what was it for? Somewhere in the back of her mind she knew it was important. After a while it dawned on her - the old music box! The one she had played with so often at her Nan's house. Much loved Nan, who smelled of baking bread and carbolic soap, with dinner-lady arms to cuddle her. Her Nan left it to her. It was nothing special. It was quite worn and ugly. The music was enchanting and evoked feelings of happiness every time she heard it. How could she forget something that held so many memories, but even more importantly, where was it now?

'The loft!... If he's taken it I'll...' she groaned, running to find the step.

This time she ascended the loft more able footed and switched on the light. It stank of dampness and dust. She scanned all around looking for anything that remained. It was empty. She balanced along one of the beams and walked to the dividing wall, brushing cobwebs on the way. Then she spun round like an oversized gymnast and followed the next beam. Still nothing! Suddenly a small ray of light shone through a hole in the roof.

Sod it! she thought. Let the Jackson's fix it! They had given her enough grief to last a lifetime, constantly making lists of work to be carried out. Demanded a reduction for the state of the fence and complaining over the curtains and the colour of the walls. It was true though, the Soon-to-be-ex liked brown.

The light fell onto the water tank. It must be a sign! she thought, slowly walking over to where it shone. Tucked away in the corner was a carrier bag containing the last and most lewd of the girlie magazines. 'Bugger!'

She slung the offending bag down through the hatch and took a cigarette from her pocket. Sitting on one of the beams she quickly inhaled, then blew the smoke out slowly. It spiraled outwards, embracing the dust particles floating in the shaft of light. 'What the - .' Something hard and cold prodded her ankle. Half hidden under the insulation-felt was the music box. The brass handle once shiny, now tarnished, summoned her to lift it from its hiding place.

Eve rekindled the bonfire in the back garden and before she could light up another cigarette Anton appeared.

'What is it you doing now luff?'

'Finishing what I've started,' she said, smiling at him.

'You finding more, dirty books, he be looking at?'

Eve nodded. 'This is the last thankfully. At least I hope so. If Pauline Jackson finds anymore I'll soon know about it.'

'I'm going to be taking rubbish to dump luff. Bin men won't be fetching on time. Seeing you later. Taking care.' He waved, then pushed his wheelbarrow down the drive. Starting a two mile walk to the tip, he sang softly in his native tongue.

She went indoors and found the recliner empty. Carefully feeling the seat before lowering herself gently into the chair. Thinking how much she'd miss Anton and his overuse of the verb intransitive.

This peculiar form of speech he'd deliberately used since his one and only operatic solo in the local church! Anton had what the Irish call a silver tenor voice. It was this gift that won Maudie over in the end. He sang Polish love songs to her as they walked on the moors.

Anton told Eve the story of how he and Maudie met after the Second World War, when he came to live in England. He and Maudie had walked out together for two years when Father Simon agreed to marry them - if she converted to Catholicism. She faithfully took instruction and Anton agreed to sing at her Confirmation.

It was all very romantic as he walked down to the altar in a borrowed dinner jacket. He took up his position. The organ struck up the first cords of "Ave Maria" and the subliminal tones of his voice rang out. The whole surprised congregation was held in the moment and Maudie's eyes shone with pride and emotion. As the final notes rang out everyone applauded. He brought the house down. Now if Anton had simply bowed and walked away all would have been well, but he decided to make a little speech. 'Father Simon, ladies and gentlemen, thank you for giving me the clap!' Before he could continue there was a ripple of laughter from the Irish sector, quiet at first then building into a crescendo. Even Father Simon had to restrain himself. Years of practise and abstinence were unable to contain the laughter rising in his throat, so he finally managed to disguise it as a coughing fit. Poor Anton puzzled and embarrassed carried on: 'I come in this church every other day and get very satisfied.' More laughter followed. 'But I come more when I meet my Maudie.' Hysteria from the folks as they stamped their feet. 'She is now a satisfied Catholic and comes all the time.' The agony of trying not to laugh at a time of great seriousness, in a place of worship, is just too much for any mere mortal to handle. A sea of heads rocked back and forth, laughing until they cried. Only Maudie looked mortified, sitting in her white chiffon outfit among the little children who had been Confirmed with her that day. Anton returned up the aisle back to Maudie's side, his speech unfinished, to thunderous applause. His face got redder in confusion.

Maudie later explained to him his little errors. His embarrassment was so great he refused to go to Mass. Then he wanted to fight all the men who'd laughed. Finally Father Simon persuaded him to return to the fold, but couldn't get him to sing solo ever again, not even at his own wedding. 'So you seeing luff,' Anton told her, 'I making sure I getting it all right all the time now!'

Smoke Gets In Your Eyes

Boxing Day moved onwards, with the usual one-sided fight over the recliner and the same old films hashed up again for the Christmas Holidays. Eve settled down in the deck chair and taking the polishing cloths from under the sink, carefully wiped down the music box. It was in a pitiful state. Most of the veneer had bubbled up, or fallen off. Pieces of inlaid ivory and mother of pearl had long since vanished leaving only an outline, defining the original picture of a dragon. Then she polished the brass handle and lock, until they glimmered once more. She had forgotten how heavy the box was and placed it down on the carpet, wondering whether the mechanism inside still worked. Slowly she raised the lid, wound the key and released the catch.

Still the bell-like chimes of the unknown tune rang out loud and clear. The music had a kind of oriental rhythm to it. She remembered how the sound always made her want to dance like a Geisha girl. She smiled, stood up and started doing a twirling movement, while opening an imaginary fan in one delicate hand movement. She took small deliberate steps and tilted her head to one side in a provocative way and lowering her eye lids. She was in ballet class again, taking her gold medal examination. Nan had made the satin costume, together with a wig fashioned from black wool, glued with Spangles sweets and sequins. The music slowed down so she went to wind it up again.

Heathcliffe pounced at her, growling and spitting in a Mrs. Rochester fit. Clung onto her legs with his claws, then did a back-flip before she could reach him. The mournful mog peed in the remaining deck chair, then leapt into the recliner, still growling.

Spiteful bastard. He knows. He does it on purpose, she thought.

His servant in an oversized shirt, leggings and leg-warmers, doing a predatory dance to howling bells, scared the hell into him. When she closed the lid he calmed down a little, then fell into a twitching sleep. She noticed the jagged edges of the scars across his head. Silvery lines where the fur hadn't regrown. 'Poor old thing,' she said, debating whether to stroke his troubled body. Then she decided against any contact.

Instead she picked up the music box in one hand and the sodden deck chair in the other and left the cat alone. "The Great Escape" flickered on the black and white television, so she left it switched on, hoping it might give 'nut case' some ideas. She left the deck chair under the running tap outside until all signs of cat-pee had dispersed, then propped it up against the wall in the garage to dry. After which she patted some Dettol on her scratches.

Carrying the heavy music box into the front bedroom she sat on the carpet. This time when she opened it, all was quiet. The top tray, once covered in green velvet was now threadbare with the wood showing through. Her medals for gymnastics and ballet had also tarnished through years of neglect.

Memories of how lithe she used to be, flooded back. She tried to balance on one leg. Then stretch out her arms above her head, upon which she crashed into the wardrobe. For the first time in years she took a long hard look at herself in the mirror. She saw her mother looking back at her. The resemblance was remarkable. She laughed out loud. Forty two years old and she'd turned into her mother.

'O.K. Big titty woman! Let's see what's happened to the rear view...' she said to the mirror.

Throwing off her shirt, leggings and leg warmers, she studied her reflection. White bra, with big pants that clung to her love handles. 'Think you can handle the full Monty?' she challenged herself. Taking a hand mirror she was dismayed to find that her backside had crept down her thighs. And what were those lumps bulging from under her bra? 'I've grown breast on my back,' she wailed. Bra and pants cast off, the grim truth hit her.

'Breathe,' she said, letting it all hang out. Now, the bad news: everything has gone to Land's End, apart from the boobs. They're floating somewhere near Doncaster. Can't fit a pencil under them...

That's a good thing... Shit! She lifted her arse to where it used to be and found a triangle of white flesh underneath. Even lying down while sunbathing, her backside had still yielded to gravity.

Positive points. Skin good. Factor 30 worked. Downside: the freckles had joined forces. Chin fine from the front, a little saggy from the side. Cheeks taut from constant fixed smile. Frown lines between eyebrows. Mental note to raise eyebrows. She tried this and finished up looking like a surprised owl. Hair still natural. No sign of grey. Conclusion: Exercise more, take up jogging. Buy a larger sport's bra. Invest in a brightly coloured track suit. Borrow video of Eva Fraser's facial workout from Sue. Stop talking to herself. Get a life!

Fifteen donkey kicks for either buttock, and ten sit-ups later she decided to cover up. The sight of her body jiggling around depressed her. She and Heathcliffe had one thing in common. In all-fours position their bellies nearly touched the floor. She put on her dressing gown and went to make hot chocolate. Bringing the biscuit tin with her to the bedroom, for comfort. Then she pressed down the clawed carpet with her foot. The cat dodged the closing door and sidled in. He raked the wallpaper behind her because he could. The Godfather of cats. Settling on the carpet she lifted the tray out from the music box.

Underneath were seven glass paperweights all different, all forgotten, covered in dust. "Mrs. Pinkerton's Bits and Bats Stall!" The old fortuneteller come bric-a-brac seller who they visited at Christmas Eve on her birthday. How could she forget this eccentric ostentatious woman.

❧

The first time she had set eyes on Mrs. Pinkerton was on her Seventh Birthday. The Christmas fair had come to town and she wanted to spend her birthday money. They all decided to visit after tea as the fairground transformed into something beautiful when it went dark; hiding the blackened factories behind the land.

Her mother loved anything remotely psychic: black cats, four leaf clovers, a rabbit's foot. She even kept a small piece of coal in her purse. So Meg, Angela, Eve and their mother went straight over to the stall, leaving Dad and Nan to visit the Boxing Booth, their favourite place, along with The Wall of Death.

31

Mrs. Pinkerton had a stork's nest of dyed black hair. Set like concrete. Her eyebrows painted on in an arch, stood a good three inches above her own greying ones. Two perfect circles of red daubed on her cheeks. The rest of her face was a white as snow. Then there was a gash of crimson for the mouth, with matching finger nails that curled under at the ends.

The first two fingers of her right hand and the tip of her thumb stained yellow from the nicotene. Her teeth the same dull colour and the bottom two centre ones were missing. A rustling dress made of purple satin, patterned with large garish flowers, set off enormous amethyst ear-rings. They fascinated Eve more than anything, jiggling around under the fairground lights as her head moved in animated conversation with her customers.

'Now lady. Don't be mean with me. I need paper money before I tell your fortune. The curse of the gypsy is strong!' she warned one terrified well-dressed woman who wearing a fox-cub choker round her neck. Eve fascinated by this poor dead animal, noticed the back legs were stitched together. The head threaded through them, with the tail dangling on her lapels. Mrs. Pinkerton seemed more sympathetic to the next woman in a coat worn at the cuffs and down at heel shoes. 'You give me a bit of lipstick love, or rouge, a cigarette even and I tell you how better things can happen for you.' The woman shook her head. Mrs. Pinkerton reached under the counter and pressed something into her hand. 'It will bring you luck. God Bless!'

'Go on Meg!' urged eleven year old Angela. 'Ask her if you'll marry Geoff!'

Mrs. Pinkerton looked up at Meg's serene face and said, 'You know your heart! Be happy now. The train did not stop for latecomers. Before long the next one arrived.' Meg gave her sixpence, but was a little disappointed, hoping for a magical sign of an engagement ring.

Angela shouted out, 'Me! Me next!' holding out her palm to the woman.

'You will always have fine things!'

'Will I know my heart too!'

'Only if you look into it pretty girl!'

'What's she know anyway! Old faggot!' sniffed Angela, linking arms with Meg and walking towards The Waltzer.

"When I was just a little girl I asked my mother what would I be...", Doris Day sang out.

'Come forward little flame-haired child. Don't be shy.'

Eve stepped nearer until she could smell the fortune-teller's perfume. "Devon Violets!" It rose above the smell of hot dogs and candy floss. Her mother wore "Evening in Paris" when she could afford it, but this perfume was stronger, almost intoxicating.

'She wants to buy something with her Birthday money, Mrs. Pinkerton,' Eve's mother told her.

'I've got the very thing for you my dove,' she said reaching under the counter.

When she opened the palm of her hand a small paperweight was nestling in the middle. Inside delicately worked chrysanthemums twinkled under the artificial lights.

'Do you like it child?'

'It lovely,' Eve sighed.

'Take it for one shilling, but... you must remember... Study the flowers' perfection and decide what you want the most, not what is best. Do you hear mother?'

Eve and her mother looked puzzled, but handed over the money. Mrs. Pinkerton wrapped the glass dome in a piece of newspaper, saying 'Now mother! What about your future.'

'I'd rather not know love. We've enough on with the threat of Atomic bombs dropped on the gas tanks - and the men being on short-time.'

'Listen mother. I tell you for free. Your blood is too hot. Cool it down! Eat mackerel and drink cabbage water.'

She nodded and thanked the fortune-teller. As they left the stall her mother grimaced at the thought, making Eve laugh, then bought candy floss for them both.

Later that evening Meg asked her mother: 'How did she know about the train not stopping?'

'She must have read it in the papers, love. Don't worry about things past. There's nothing we can do about it now.'

Meg was always serene and gentle. She attracted the attention of every male in the village with these qualities - and at fourteen years old bore a striking resemblance to Ava Gardner. She had her father's dark eyes. Ron Halliwell was completely smitten at first sight and spent most of his wages on a new suit to impress her. She liked his soft voice. He didn't shout like the rougher lads who lived over the boundary. He was quite shy in the beginning and she wondered if he really liked her. They had been walking out together for four weeks, when she asked: 'Don't you fancy me?'

'Oh! Yes! More than anybody in the world!'

'Well why don't you want to kiss me then?'

Ron kissed her gently and put his arm round her waist. Now they were really girlfriend and boyfriend.

He lived in Highbank, the other side of the bridge, at the top of the hill. The Rotherham village where the sisters lived, nestled in a valley. In front of a line of steel-works and electrode factories, there was a scattering of pylons, surrounded by a fringe of woods. The village had the apt name of Blackridge. With its smoking chimneys rising out of the gloom, that marred the view from the higher woodlands.

After taking only six paces under the bridge, the villagers stood in Sheffield. Meg and the other kids from the Youth Club often joked about this. 'I'm going to Sheffield tonight,' they'd say, then run under the bridge.

Ron was on his way home from work, when he saw Meg and the other kids playing under the bridge. She wore a blue sail cloth dress, which clung to her hourglass figure. It was love at first sight. He couldn't believe his luck when she said she would 'go out' with him.

Meg winced when she remembered the last time they'd kissed. He promised to marry her when she was sixteen. He saved every penny up for the engagement ring. It was in his pocket when they found the body on that oppressive day.

A day when a thunderous gathering of anvil shaped clouds, held in their grip the smell of the factories. The pylons crackled as the static of the forthcoming storm built up to breaking point. Then the monsoon began, pounding up from the pavements like bullets, washing the filth in rivulets down the drains. The crackles of fork lightening, illuminating the dark woods. The river banks burst and flash-flooded. Black rain spilled out under the bridge, filling the road with deep sludge and sewage from the riverbed. All traffic cut off and rerouted.

The only way home was a mile walk over to the canal bridge, or to leg it over the railway lines behind the electrodes' factory. There were no level crossing gates, just planks of wood and a signal in the distance, showing red or green. Most of the workers took the short cut at some time, hurrying to get home and get rid of the stink on their bodies. Covered in the graphite dust, they were unrecognizable coming out into the dark, showing only the whites of their eyes.

One after another they ran across the lines, chancing it when the signal changed. Ron was the last, busy showing the foreman the ring he'd bought. He'd let the boy sneak out at break time to the jewelers, after the pay packets were handed out. Ron said his farewells, drenched to the skin as the rain hailed down, streaking the muck into his eyes. He didn't see the train until it hit him. It sliced off his head and dragged his body for half a mile before it stopped.

After the rains ceased a stillness hung over the village. It wasn't as if tragedy was unfamiliar to them. Men were often brutally injured and maimed in the factories. A man had fallen into the smelting bosch and died instantly. But young Ron's death was too terrible for them to comprehend. All of the folks united in grief. A full turn out packed the little church on the hill. Ron's mother collapsed at the funeral. She was the one who identified her youngest son's body.

Meg was devastated but didn't let her sorrow show. She kept it inside and never uttered a word about the event. To her it would have been a betrayal of his memory. She needed to think of him as he was, smiling and quiet. She wore the ring on a chain around her neck, until she met Geoff. She still has it in her jewelry box along with a photograph of a skinny blonde youth with a shy grin.

Downtown

Eve recalled how much she had treasured her first paperweight, staring at it for hours under the light, marveling at its intricacy. When her teacher, Miss Johnson, suggested she enter a painting competition sponsored by a London Tea Company, she knew immediately what she would paint.

The child draped her mother's purple velvet scarf on the blue checked table-cloth and placed the paperweight in the middle. She studied the light reflecting in the dome and considered how to catch it, to illuminate the flowers deep in the centre. When she finished her painting she left it to dry on the table.

'Come and look at this Stan, what our Evie has painted.'

Her father looked in amazement at the richly coloured picture. The chrysanthemums, his favourites, seem to dance on the paper.

'It's almost like a photograph, only better,' he said.

She overheard her parents praise that night and always remembered it. Sometimes they forgot to say good things to her. Things they often said to her sisters. Like the times her Dad called Meg, 'Ava Gardner', or 'Film Star'. She loved her big sister dearly and knew how beautiful Meg was because all the boys whistled whenever they saw her.

Later when Angela started to develop she was 'Doris Day,' because of her sunny smile and blonde hair. Eve couldn't wait for her turn to enter the mysterious world of womanhood, wondering what her Film Star name would be. For now though she was content with 'Little One'.

When she won the painting competition in London a simple form was sent to her parents for them to sign. 'Eve Watts will/will not be able to attend the prize giving in London on 28th January.'

Miss Johnson had written on the bottom of the slip. 'If Eve cannot attend on the day, unfortunately, the first prize will go to the runner-up.'

Just as soon as her parents found out that they had to cover their own traveling expenses to collect the prize they told Miss Johnson they needed to think about the matter.

'What's to do Stan? We can't afford to send her to London and she can't go on her own. One of us will have to go with her.'

'We'll manage Rose. Don't worry. There's that money in the tea caddie...'

'But that's for our Angela's tap shoes, and a new winter coat. She's had her heart set on that red coat with the fur collar and it's been 'put by' at Mrs. Brocklehurst's shop...What's the prize anyway? Is it money?'

'She's won a First Prize Certificate. Imagine Rose, she's only seven and has beat hundreds of kids from all over the country, some nine and ten years old.'

'Can't they post it?'

'The newspapers will be there and they want a photo of the winner. You know, publicity for the Tea Company.'

'Well! You can be the one to tell 'lady' the bad news, because I'm not!'

When Angela was told that she might not get the red coat, but Evie could go to London with the money, she started to cry and didn't stop for two days. Eve couldn't bear to hear her sister sniffling through the night.

'Dad?' she said the next morning. 'It doesn't matter, you know, about me going to London. Mum said it's such a long way to go just to get a bit of paper.'

'Evie love are you sure? It's a 'First Prize' certificate and you'll get your photo in the papers as well.'

'Honest Dad. It doesn't matter. I can still paint can't I?'

'Course you can,' he said, kissing the top of her head. 'I'll go and tell our Angela to stop bawling.'

They didn't mention the event again. Eve simply took the sealed envelope back to her teacher with the 'will' crossed out, hiding her disappointment.

For months after she really believed if she said: 'Shazzam,' in the right way, she could fly to London and explain everything. Get her prize. Have her photo taken. Be famous - almost. Standing on the edge of the curb, arms pointing skyward with a tea towel for a cape, she uttered the word over and over:

'Shazzam...Shazarnmmm...Shzm...Zaashaammm.... Masshazzzz...Shaaazzam...Shazzzam...Shazzaaam... Shhhhaaazzaam!'

In the end she accepted that Captain Marvel was far more powerful.

છ૭

She put out her hand to stroke Heathcliffe, who had stretched out next to her. He purred softly. Looked almost docile. His claws lashed out. Shit-head wins every time, she thought.

Mrs. Pinkerton's words came back to her: "Decide what you want the most, not what is best." She wondered what would have happened if her Dad had insisted on her going. If he realized how important it was to her. Picking up the delicate paperweight she looked deep into the centre. The flowers seemed more open than they used to be, and she yawned, exhausted from the last few months anguish.

She was woken with a jolt and the sound of heavy doors slamming and a whooshing of steam. 'Come on Evie love. We got to find our way to the underground... Excuse me mate. How do we get to this Art Gallery?' her father asked, pointing at the map.

'You go down the steps and carry on until you come to the ticket office. Get tickets for Sloane Square, changing at Earl's Court. Then you'll find a bus stop outside the tube and it'll drop you just across from the gallery.'

'Thanks mate!'

Stan was as excited as Eve. He'd never been to London before, in fact the furthest he traveled was to the East Coast. Everything was so noisy and confusing. They were dressed in their Sunday best and Evie carried the 'packing up' Mum had made them. Ham sandwiches, Nan's jam scones, and a flask of tea.

After Stan got the tickets they both went through the barrier gate together, laughing when they got stuck. The wooden escalator was even more fun.

'Don't look down Evie,' he said, feeling dizzy and holding onto her hand.

When they finally found the art gallery, after many wrong directions, it was full of chattering children and proud parents. As Stan handed the doorman their invitation he raised his eyebrows and shouted over to the curator. 'She's here sir!'

Every head turned to look at Eve. She felt very nervous and blushed crimson.

'So this is the seven year old who paints like an angel,' he said, smiling.

Stan was very proud.

'Aye - and she can do a good likeness of her sisters, as well.'

The party was ushered into a large room with chairs set out in rows. 'Don't be afraid Eve. This is what you want the most, isn't it?' the curator said, winking at her.

There were three paintings on display, all beautifully framed and resting on stands. Eve's painting set in the middle with a gold rosette attached. When everyone had settled down in the chairs, the winners were announced in reverse order. Then it was Eve's turn to collect her certificate. Her father clapped and whistled loudly as the cameras flashed. She was handed an envelope containing a gold embossed certificate and a large white five pound note.

Later, as they were leaving, the curator said to Eve, 'Remember, if you study hard maybe one day your paintings will hang on these hallowed walls. Take this as a little gift,' he said, giving Eve a polished wooden box full of oil paints.

'Don't worry sir. I'll make sure she carries on painting,' her father replied.

'Angela can have her new coat and the tap shoes now Dad!'

'Aye, that she can love, with some to spare!'

'Why are the walls hollowed, Dad?'

'Hallowed love. It means special.'

The ham sandwiches tasted wonderful on their return journey home and as the train carriage rocked from side to side it seemed to clatter out: 'She's got first prize She's got first prize.'

The most awful wailing noise startled Eve from her dreaming. Heathcliffe was scratching up the bedroom carpet and wanted to go out. The foul fiend didn't chase her down the stairs, as usual, but began sharpening his claws on the music box, then decided to poo inside the fitted wardrobe for good measure.

Bastard!

Handbags And Gladrags

Just as she started to clean up the mess, the phone rang. It was Mavis and Shirley reminding her about their night out. They were coming over from Whinstone to go to the Boxing Day Show at the local nightclub. A taxi had been arranged to bring them over and take them back, as Eve was short on beds.

'Are you getting ready for a night of unbridled passion?' Shirl asked.

'In Maccleton? Chance would be a fine thing.'

The tickets were purchased weeks ago and Eve had completely forgotten about "A Night of Mystery with Hypnotist: Sean Mc. Shane" and supporting acts of "Liver Sounds," followed by disco and free cocktail. Shirley had questioned what sounds her liver makes, until Eve pointed out that it should have read "Liverpuddlian Sounds." Eve had lived in Derbyshire twenty five years and never set foot inside The Blue Lagoon nightclub. She really didn't feel up to going, but couldn't get out of it. She hoped her friends weren't expecting too much.

Mavis snatched the phone from Shirl. 'Get yourself dolled up love. We'll get shagged tonight if it kills us!'

'See you about nine, so don't be late,' Shirl added. 'The taxis here...We're on our way!'

Panic followed by chaos. Heathcliffe wanted feeding and followed her everywhere, trying to scratch her legs. After a quick shower, she found out the black halter neck dress bought for her fortieth birthday. All her tights had runs in them, thanks to the mad cat. Unfortunately the only unsullied leg coverings were the black stockings Mitch had given her last Christmas, with bows and diamonds on the ankles. They would have to suffice, hoping she'd not thrown away the suspender belt. She found it in the second drawer still in the foil wrapper. It was too late to buy replacement tights. She fasten the belt and clipped the stocking into place. Black suspenders peering beneath big white pants did not look good. Searching for the black suede court shoes, she found them under the heap of flatties.

She quickly put in the heated rollers to tame the frizz, then poked her eye with the mascara stick in her desperate hurry to be ready on time. After washing out her contact lens and redoing her left eye, which was decidedly redder than the right one, a final flourish of peach lipstick was added, just as the door-bell rang.

She ran down the stairs, saying: 'Two minutes,' then realized she'd still got the rollers in. A quick untangling, leaving red hair inside the spikes, followed by a swift brushing out, she grabbed her coat and bag and slammed the door. Applying more lipstick on the way.

Her mother's voice echoed in the back of her mind. Never go out without lipstick and always put on a good face, no matter how awful you're feeling. She and Meg had learned to do this over the years. No matter what. Only Angela wasn't afraid to scrunge up her eyes and bawl. In fact Eve's neighbours thought she was handling things very well. Being dumped for a younger woman after 25 years of marriage and not so much as a broken window in anger.

They noticed no matter what hour she arrived home from work she still had time for a friendly word and a smile. She found herself smiling at dogs, even the scruffy flee bitten mongrels. It became a fixed grin. She often wondered what the Mona Lisa was thinking under that smile. Had her mother told her to put on a good face? Did she get a stiff neck and a numb backside?

'She'll soon get another man,' they said. 'She's always pleasant and compliant and men like that. Something to grab hold of. Quietly spoken. Nice walk. Not a miserable cow full of self pity, like that Irene Johnson.' Was she really a 'yielding woman?' she puzzled, thinking of "Far from the Madding Crowd." If only they knew how she really felt. Shitty summed it up pretty well.

Shirley opened the taxi door and pulled her inside. 'What's that in your hair lass ? You're a bit old for hair slides!'

Eve felt her hair and took out a forgotten roller, dropping it into her bag. The two friends fell about laughing. The girls always made her feel better. The party had already started as Shirl took a swig from a vodka bottle. She had become an expert on nightclub prices and regularly brought a very large handbag for her own booze. As always, she was dressed in red. A big boned girl with a large round face and tiny features enfolded in fat. Fake tan, with matching orange tights - and palms. Blue twinkle eye shadow. Her small bright eyes shone with excitement as she reapplied red lipstick to her mouth, teeth and cheeks.

Mavis was the opposite to Shirl. She was a petite bottle-blonde, going on fifty, dressed in her daughter's white ra-ra skirt, black boob-tube and white stilettos. In a mellow light she looked like a teenager, until the sun hit her face. Her sarcastic ex said she looked like Rod Stewart. Her on-off boyfriend, a 'flabby-faced lad' who worked in Finance, had bought her a white cony fur coat for Christmas and it was shedding like mad over the taxi's seat. 'Here, save some of that for me!' she shouted snatching the bottle from Shirl.

Mavis grinned a slash of shocking pink lipstick at the driver. Through his mirror she couldn't see he weighed about twenty stone and looked like a hippo's arse. She was extremely short-sighted and refused to do anything about it. That's why every man looked like Remington Steele, especially when she'd had a few. Maybe it was easier that way. A soft focus world where everything looked rosy. The edges blurred. Nevertheless when her driving instructor arrived, every lunch-time, to collect her for a lesson, everyone in The Civic Buildings in Ecclesham ran for cover.

Eve noticed her friend's panda eyes and wondered how she ever managed to get her mascara in the right place. Every single lash was curled with thick blobs of black. Apparently she'd bought some magnifying specs with drop down lens. She always put her make-up on with a trowel, but men seemed to find the total effect alluring.

It was because of this allure that Shirl got her fair share of the leftover men on their nights out together. She didn't mind that she always got the 'losers,' as long as she wasn't left on the shelf at the end of the evening. Like the poor cow who had to pay for her own taxi home, with nothing but a cup of Horlicks to keep her warm. Eve fitted into this category, according to the 'Gospel of Shirl,' and it was her mission to fix her friend up with more than a warming drink at bedtime. After all there were plenty of men to go round for a bit of fun, that is, 'if ginger would let herself go a bit.'

The nightclub was all and more than expected. It had a kind of jungle feel to it, with camouflage nets and plastic exotic foliage poking out everywhere. Painted black walls for intimacy had folks tripping up and crashing into each other. Red plush velvet seats around the stage, with tasseled table lamps to match, completed the effect. Tart meets Action Man sprang to mind.

After checking in their coats, they all headed for the 'Ladies' and Mavis got out their supply of alcohol. 'Go and fetch a large bottle of tonic Shirl and three glasses. It'll last longer that way, until we pull,' she ordered her friend. Then back combed her hair to make herself look taller.

The baby- faced young girls with Kim Wilde layered perms, were dressed in jump suits and headbands, and pixie leather boots that crumpled round the ankles. Eve had contemplated buying a jump suit, but changed her mind, when she worked out the logistics of having a pee. The whole top section had to swing somewhere round the hips, while the pants rested in between. Wet toilet floors were the ultimate deterrent.

'Here Evie, get some of this down your neck. It'll loosen you up a bit. Make you forget your troubles,' she giggled.

From experience Eve knew that it had the opposite effect on her, so she took a short sip and passed the bottle back. Spirits depressed her and the 'House Red' tasted like vinegar. The ladies waited in a queue to be directed to their table. Eve felt a cold glass pressed against her bare back. Turning round in shock, she saw a Seventies time-warp winking at her. He wore a brown pin-striped suit nipped in at the waist. Padded shoulders, wide trousers with turns up resting above platform boots, were offset by a flapping-collared mustard shirt and orange kipper tie. The whole ensemble clashed terribly with his acne.

The girls settled in with chicken in a basket, before the lights went down. Sean Mc. Shane was the first act, after the warm up comedian failed miserably. One of those terrible deaths that only the brave few survived. Richie Jardiner always liked to finish his comedy act with a song. Pub singer he wasn't. He was worse. It was at the poignant moment when the last strangled cord of "Please release me and let me love again..." came out of Richie's throat, and just before the sympathy applause started, someone shouted: 'CUNT!'

The Master of Ceremonies, Reg Ainsley, couldn't prize himself out of his chair quick enough to introduce the 'Star Turn.' So Sean, always anxious to begin, ran on stage as Richie did a hasty retreat. The hypnotist had to get back home to Manchester before daybreak. Ritchie's swan-song had succeeded where the comedy failed. The audience laughed hysterically. Sean leaned into the microphone and tried to sound throaty: 'Ladies and gentlemen, can I ask for some volunteers please.' A nasal whine was all he managed.

Usually a hushed silence ensued, until someone well out of it, pushed onto the stage by their drunken friends, made a fool of himself. This wasn't the case with Mavis and Shirl. They were both up there like lightning, as the drums rolled.

'It's "Little and Large", ladies and gentlemen,' Sean laughed. The audience jeered through a halo of smoke.

The nightclub had opened early, by special license for a Stag Party. The drunken bachelors near the front were baying for blood.

'Come on love,' he said peering into the dark. 'Yes you over there with your hand on that man's crotch. Don't be shy...' One of the bouncers pulled the poor girl and her boyfriend onto the stage.

After a few suggestions to the participants: that their hands were stuck together and they couldn't move their legs, he finally succeeded in hypnotizing eight people. This was six more than usual, and two of them were his relations. Sean swayed from side to side, then held onto the microphone for support. He'd actually done it, he thought. Bloody miracle. Fuck! Now what? He'd not learned how to undo the trance. Only got to page 20 in the manual. What if they sued? Bugger it. He could always change his name. The bailiffs were due any time. Sod it! He'd change his address for good measure.

Eve looked on in amazement at Mavis and Shirl, whose eyes were glazed over, with their hands in praying positions. Sean was in a state of shock, then gathered his senses. Linch Mob sprang to mind. The show must go on.

'Now then blondie. I bet you're a right little raver?' Sean said, trying not to shake.

Mavis nodded.

'Can you sing?'

She shook her head, peering soft-eyed into the audience. She grinned vacantly.

'Tonight you are Lulu and you're going to give us a song called "Shout" every time you hear this music.'

To Eve's surprise Mavis began to belt out a good imitation of the gravel-voiced Scot.

'She's a plant,' the man on the next table said to Eve, prodding her arm with his fork. She smiled. 'And that big lass next to her...it's a fella...his stooge.' She choked on her tonic water.

The unfortunate couple had worse to come. She aped a stripper doing a snake dance, and he had to look for his lost willy every time the music for "Searching," played. The poor lad ran around all night crying out: 'Have you seen my willy?' When he returned to normal his girlfriend tried to strip down to her undies, to the raunchy music. Both swore they'd not been hypnotized.

Now it was Shirl's turn. She was Margot Fonteyn dancing "Swan Lake" on points. Poor Shirl was hilarious. Her music alternated with a chap who made believe he was a sargeant major in the army. He got really mad when some youths wouldn't salute and stand to attention in the toilets.

Shirl trod on a few people's feet and knocked over a table full of drinks. Another unfortunate man did handstands, accompanied by drum rolls, while his mate tried to kiss every girl in sight when he heard: "Kiss me Honey Honey..." The former got a blinding headache and the latter his face slapped many times.

At the end of Sean's act, the band played one deliberate tune after another and caused chaos in the auditorium. Sean Mc. Shane got a standing ovation and £200. He'd spend a quarter of it on petrol before he got home. He told the audience the affect of hypnosis wears off after an hour. It didn't! Mavis developed a liking for haggis and Shirl insisted on feeding the swans every lunch-time. Heaven knows what happened to the rest of the victims.

'Now ladies and gentlemen if you could make your way quietly to the disco area, while we clean up the mess. You will be entertained by "Liver Sounds," a group of people who were nearly famous.'

Mavis was first on the dance floor. A crowd of 'Derbyshire Hardies' started to laugh. All that could be seen was her white shoes, the skirt, her hair and the bits of fur glowing on the black boob-tube. 'It's the bloody invisible woman,' one lad said. She jiggled her shoulders in a jerky kind of way, grinning at the shadowy males around the perimeter, hoping one of them was half decent looking.

'Nay! It's Minnie Mouse,' his stocky friend guffawed.

Then as the music changed she started to belt out: 'You know you want to shout...' The youth sidled over and began dancing behind her, basking in her glory, as she wildly shook her body.

"Liver Sounds" looked remarkably like the previous band, but now wore mop-head wigs and monkey suits. And just as Shirl got chatting to a bald man with a horseshoe moustache, they played Dance of the Signets again. She pirouetted round the dance floor crashing into the dancers and then stopped suddenly when the music changed, looking very puzzled. Fortunately the bald man found her and bought her a rum and coke. Mavis and the stocky lad were doing the 'Hippy Shake'.

'Do you want to dance "Red"?' A good looking youth with a gold earring, asked Eve. He was wearing a brilliant white shirt, black pants and smelled of 'Lynx' after-shave. Before she could refuse he took her by the hand and led her onto the dance floor. He moved really well. His strong thighs filled his trousers. Shirl shouted to Mavis to have a look at the hunk dancing with Eve. Mavis came over for closer inspection and got jealous. She usually got the best looking blokes and started to dance provocatively, next to him. Spinning out her Ra-Ra skirt and giving him the come on. He ignored her and started smooching with Eve.

Eve relaxed and enjoyed herself. He bought her a Gin and Tonic and she felt herself unwinding. She celebrated her birthday and Christmas at last. Felt her youthful optimism returning. When he suggested they go outside from some fresh air, she actually agreed. She'd already seen her friends leave through the fire doors.

'I've got a thing for red hair. Yours is tussled and tawny. Turns me on... It suggests: passion, fire and heat,' he said, nibbling her ear.

She'd not heard that before and was quite flattered. The nicest compliment a man had paid her was: 'pre-Raphaelite,' and it was from the eighty years old vicar. The youth was a good kisser too, not overpowering. He worked his way gently from her ears, to her neck and then her breasts, before taking her mouth with an ardent intensity she'd not experienced before. At last a man who knows what he doing, she thought. Praise heaven. She started to kiss him back and felt a wave of heat rush through her body, despite the freezing cold night. When he pinned her against the wall and tried to raise her skirt above her waist, she drew the line. He lost it. Pressing his hardness against her, rubbing her suspenders.

'That's enough!' she shouted. 'COOL IT!' then pushed him away. Particularly not wanting anyone to catch sight of the black suspenders and white pants. Sex was the last thing on her mind when she had dressed.

'Come on love. You know you want it...How long has it been old girl?' he asked, still pressing into her with his growing bulge.

'What?' she said, stunned.

'That's what you older women come here for. Isn't it?...To get fucked because the old man's not up to it anymore.'

'YOU CONCEITED SHIT-HEAD!' she shouted, getting angry for the third time that year.

'Come on. You know you'll give in, in the end,' he said, trying to push her down onto the floor.

'Can't you take NO for an answer? And will you get your paws off me!'

Before he could move another inch, a great fat fist came down on top of his head and buckled him at the knees.

'You heard the lady! Now bog off sonny-boy! Go and play with your toys,' the taxi driver said, helping Eve up off the floor.

'Don't want a granny anyway,' he shouted sulkily, going back through the fire doors.

'You all right love?' the big man asked.

'Yes thanks...Serves me right for drinking,' she said shakily lighting a cigarette.

'Can I take you back home? he added. Then noticing her expression, said: 'Strictly business. I mean as a cab-fare.'

'Please...I'll get my coat. What about my friends?'

'They're over there, in the rocking steamed-up Capri, doing a synchronized shag... They want me to come back for them in an hour.'

Traveling through the winding Derbyshire lanes, only the headlights lit up the pitch blackness. She was on her way back to a cup of Horlicks, feeling annoyed and, at the same time, pleased with herself. Annoyed for leading the youth on - and at herself for wanting him. But at the same time pleased she'd stood up to him. The big man's intervention had saved Lothario from a swift kick to the groin with a stiletto. A deal more painful that a blow to the head.

The last time she'd lost her temper was when the school bully George Swift, had beaten Vee, her best friend, mercilessly. He forced her to take her knickers down behind the bike shed. Eve was incensed when she saw her friend cowering in fear, and him leering at her. His fists still clenched in case she disobeyed him. Eve jumped onto his back and pulled her hair out in handfuls, clawing his eyes at the same time, yelling: 'Keep your hands off my friend!'

George was a stocky lad and punched her around the head, until she let go. Undeterred she returned blow for blow, in the way her dad had shown her. Making a fist, folding her thumb over her fingers and pushing hard from the shoulder. She received a few bruises in the process, but in the end he backed off, when he caught one, fair and square right in the eye. She remembered Vee saying in admiration, as they were led back to the classroom: 'Holy Moly! The redhead's come out of her shell.'

Neither of them told Mr. Marsh what had happened. He must have guessed because George had to go for a caning from Mr. Barker, the Head Teacher. He came back in tears. It was the only time Mr. Marsh hadn't dished out his own punishment. Eve thought she would get the ruler on her hand, but instead she and Vee were treated kindly by the school nurse. They told their parents they'd fallen into some blackberry bushes. It was easier that way. The bully had been shamed by a girl half his size, and that was the end of it.

Ray, the taxi-driver dropped her off safe and sound outside her door, refusing any payment. 'Don't worry about it, me duck,' he said in his soft Derbyshire accent. 'Your friend's new beaus will pay me... Merry Christmas love and a Happy New Year...Why is it always the nice people who get hurt?' he added, reversing into the drive and turning on his Barry Manilow tape.

'I don't know Ray. I really don't. Maybe it's because nice equals daft in these parts...Merry Christmas and a Happy New Year and... Thanks.'

What's New Pussycat

The Soon-to-be-ex hated animals and they reciprocated the emotion. Maybe it was the lingering smell of embalming fluid. Even the family thought it stemmed from something connected to his line of work. Angela called him 'The Embalmer', or 'The Mummy'. Eve always defended him saying he put poor souls to rest while making them as attractive as possible. Old Gran had finally accepted him full time, into the family funeral business, Crookshank's Emporium of Peace, because she could no longer cope with humping all the bodies about on her own.

Eve was convinced his inability to demonstrate affection was a safeguard, a way of distancing himself from any emotion. A device to save him from getting hurt. At an early age, forced to carry out embalming procedures, he simply pretended the corpses weren't real. And so this disassociation from reality spilled over into his relationships. No one could reach him, except through anger, then he clamped up completely and sought cold revenge. The only genuine love he'd known was that shown by herself and her mother. Unable to return these acts of unconditional kindness, which he saw as weakness, he developed sarcastic responses instead.

After his mother had been forced to leave home pregnant and unmarried, Old Gran cut her out of her life. He was born in a home for 'Wayward Girls,' where the expectant mothers were interred and treated like criminals. Forced to scrub floors until the skin peeled away from their fingers. Daily told they would got to hell, by the nuns. Knowing that as soon after their babies were born they would be taken. It was usually in the night when it happened. Secreted the infants away and given to the adoptive parents. Everything swept under the carpet. Hypocrisy replaced honesty. On the day of the proposed adoption, she escaped with the child. She'd planned it for weeks, noting the slack period, when the nuns had lunch.

An elderly couple found her in the bus station, crying her eyes out. They took pity on them. Became guardians and gave them both a home. She named the child Mitcham after the film-star Robert. Earning money from the only work experience she had: flower arranging.

He told Eve that his mother died at the age of nineteen from Polio, after spending a year in an 'iron lung,' her muscles wasting away. And that the only way she could look at her baby was through a mirror above her head, unable to hold him. Her benefactors contacted the child's Grandmother. Old Gran had returned all her daughter's letters unopened, so they were able to trace the child's only relatives.

Old Gran, vindictive as ever, refused to open the door, but her husband let them in. His heart melted he saw the blonde child, the image of his daughter. He relented and said they would take care of him. Of course Old Gran never did! A nurse was hired to bring him up until he was ten years old. Then Old Gran set him to work in the funeral emporium at weekends. When her husband died barking mad, Mitch became the hen-pecked man of the house. She controlled all 6'2" of him, even choosing his clothes, right down to his white Y-fronts from Doncaster market.

Years later when Old Gran had shuffled off her mortal coil, Mitch came home late one night wearing gardening gloves, clinging on to a howling filthy moggie - and blood pouring from his face. Eve couldn't believe her eyes. The cat lived in the box bedroom with a lit tray and ample food, for the first few weeks. The only way she could change the lit tray, was to hold him down under a fishing net. If she could catch him. Many times he tried to bolt out of the house, but she knew Mitch would never forgive her if the cat went missing. And he seemed rather fond of the battle-scarred demon, so she tried to keep the peace. Nursing her injuries in silence.

'Where did you find him?' she asked one night, as the cat growled at her.

He laughed sheepishly: 'He sort of found me!'

Mitch had been scoffing down double Mac. Donald's cheese burgers in the car, after a late game of snooker. In the winter he played snooker, and in the summer golf, until the glorious twelfth. Dead animals and birds skinned in the garage, were sold to his friends as organic.

That evening the back window of the car, left open to let out the tell tale smell, beckoned a ferel cat. Mitch knew Eve would have his dinner ready, but he could always manage two meals. His Gran had always scrimped on the food. He thought of the many times he'd put three Wheetabix under his corn-flakes, to soak up all the milk, knowing his Granddad would get the blame, and smiled.

He was just about to tackle the second burger when this howling flea-bag jumped onto his shoulder, dug in its claws and snatched the burger, before leaping into the back seat. When Mitch tried to move the cat towards the window it bit his hand. For some inexplicable reason he liked the mad mog. He felt an instant affinity with it. Its fur was dull, the left ear was missing and on its head and down its back were livid scars, as if it had been hit by something heavy and sharp. Battle scarred Heathcliffe, he thought. An apt choice of name. Mitch decided there and then, that the cat needed him, when really, it was he who needed the cat!

He carefully leaned over and wound up the back window of the old yellow Ford Anglia. Before driving to the all night Supermarket, giving the cat the rest of his chips to keep it quiet. He stocked up on cat food and biscuits, got a tray and a huge bag of litter, together with cat shampoo! He laughed thinking about how to get the cat into the bath. He also bought worm tablets and flea powder, medicated wipes and a collar with a bell on!

Walking to the gardening section he bought a large fishing net and some heavy duty gardening gloves. The girl at the check-out advised him on how to get the pills into the cat. So he also bought a pair of Wellingtons and a dark coloured towel! 'You see, you have to wrap the cat tightly in the towel, then drop him into the wellington and he wont be able to move, then you can pop the tablet in his mouth. You have to hold his jaws together though, or he'll spit it out!' Again Mitch laughed!

That night it took all his strength to keep the struggling cat in the bath while Eve washed him carefully with the shampoo. They both had raised scars on their arms, but bravely continued with what they'd started. A suicide mission!

'Just hold on,' Eve said, having an idea. 'If I fill the bath with more water, he'll be completely covered, then it'll wash the scar on his back.'

As the bath filled up the mog started to do a catty-paddle, still growling and rolling its eyes.

'That's the easy bit!' said Eve, pulling out the plug. As the water swirled down the plug-hole, a residue of drowned fleas and grime was left behind.

'Yowwwwllllll!' The wild cat clawed its way up Mitch's arm and soaked him through. Eve tried to wrap him in the towel, but he spat at her and raked her hand.

'Get the fishing net!' Mitch wailed, as the cat, punctured it ways round his neck.

After about fifteen minutes of chaos, they managed to catch the soggy mog with the net. He became still, mewling softly. Resigned to his fate. He was patted dry inside the net and then released into the small bedroom, onto a carpet covered in the "Daily Mail", just in case of accidents. From that moment the mad cat ruled the roost. Showed them what's what. They never tried the towel and Wellington trick, leaving the worm dosing and check up to the poor vet, who gave Heathcliffe a jab in the back of the neck to sedate him.

Christmas Aint Like Christmas Anymore

27th December.

Eve felt more optimistic and decided to tidy up the garden at the request of the Jacksons. Wrapping up warmly she tried to turn over the hard ground. The dying embers of gussets and magazines were raked into the soil beneath. Then she attempted to dig round the edges of the lawn to give it some sort of definition. The feature in the centre of the lawn was Mitch's first and last attempt at sculpture.

Ma Winters next door, had watched his every move from her bedroom window. She was known as 'The Twitcher' not because of her love of birds. Far from it. Any activity from her neighbours, would result in her net curtains twitching around. Although she did have the eyesight of a hawk. She treated acts of kindness from Eve, with suspicion, thinking the younger woman was after her money. But she still let Eve cut her grass, run errands and Spring clean for her, while her only son stayed well away.

She did all these good turns, because it was her nature to be helpful. That was the way in her village. The more she did, the more the woman demanded. Mitch told his wife she was born to serve. Maybe he had a point, she thought. The happiest she'd been since marrying him was her first job in the NHS as a trainee Cardiographer. She felt useful, comforting the patients wired up and earthed to the bed for each reading. Most of them were miners. Shy about taking their shirts off in front of 'a bit o' a lass.' Making excuses for their backs covered in black scars. Slivers of coal embedded under the skin. Looked like jagged tattoos. She remembered telling the men to wear them with pride. A talisman to hard graft.

The husband on the other hand, had delusion that he was a hero, reading all the 'Flashman' books to encourage this idea. While Ma Winters reminisced about her glory days in South Africa, when she had black servants. A pair of deuces. Two of a kind.

It was only when Anton told Eve how two-faced the 'Bobby wooman' was, that she stopped being general dog's-body. Apparently Ma Winters and Minnie Winters, her sister-in-law, had called Eve a 'blind fool' to Maudie. And that she wasn't beautiful enough, or clever enough to hold on to her husband. Maudie told Anton, then Anton told Eve. Unbeknown to Eve he threw rotten eggs at Ma Winters' front window, the next dark night. She asked Eve to clean the mess. She didn't.

So when the old busy-body saw Mitch working in the garden for the first time she got very jealous, until she saw the result of his labour. Then the whole street knew about 'the water feature.'

The husband had got a promotion at school and decided to do something creative in the garden. He didn't know a dandelion from a dahlia. He was only familiar with lilies. So anything horticultural was out of the question. Anybody could mix a bit of concrete, he thought. Some of the brown emulsion paint left over from the lounge, was added to the mixture. It started out as a fountain and ended up looking like the sludge mound Richard Dreyfuss obsessed over in "Close Encounters…" He'd gone indoors to watch the golf on television. The concrete set too quickly and he gave up his one and only endeavor in the garden. He simply blanked out the mound, as if it didn't exist.

As Eve stretched out her back and aching buttocks, from the donkey kicks, Anton peered over the fence. 'What you be doing, you stupid wooman!' he shouted climbing over. 'Here, be giving me the fork. It being man's work doing gardening… I getting rid of "Shit Mountain",' he added, snatching the implement from her hands.

Eve smiled at him and went indoors to put the kettle on. Then she heard the sound of the heavy hammer smashing the concrete, along with rhythmic swearing. Two mugs of hot tea and a plate of mince pies were placed on the garden wall. Anton took out a small bottle of brandy from his dungarees and poured a liberal amount into each mug. 'Good health luff!' he chuckled, 'and maying the bastard's balls be dropping off!' She couldn't help laughing.

Soon the garden looked almost landscaped as the little man, strong as a ox, forced the soil to yield under the fork. He painted the smashed pieces of concrete white and made a rockery. Then pushed a few of his own plants in between the gaps. He dead-headed the rosebushes and hydrangeas to finish it off.

Her father's hydrangeas were always sky blue and as big as dinner plates. She dug the bushes out of his Allotment and brought them to Derbyshire. Something to remind her of him. They didn't like the soil. Tiny blossoms of a mangy purplish pink followed. Watered often and fed with iron filings, tea and manure, didn't work.

'That being better luff...You wanting to coming inside and having some roast beef and Yorkshire pudding with me?' he asked, wiping his brow.

'Are you sure? That would be very nice.'

'It being better than very nice. It being bloody fantastic! I cooking many times in Poland, making rabbit tasting like beef. My Grandmother she keeping chickens, so sometimes we eating plenty good. Not like when Germans coming. Bastards! They taking everything and -...Many dying!' he said angrily.

Eve freshened up and changed her clothes. Walking round to Anton's house she wondered in what state it would be. She hadn't been inside since Maudie died and was surprised to find it clean and fresh. But she'd never seen so much clutter. On every step there were: bags, shoes, boxes, even bottles. The sitting room was stacked high with papers and books. A vast collection of plastic cartons were balanced on top of the kitchen units. It was as if he needed to fill every empty space with reminders of Maudie.

'Be coming in and sitting down at table luff! I cutting meat up after I washing hands!' He'd changed into the white shell-suit she'd bought him for Christmas. She knew he hated it. It rustled around when he moved. She also knew he would send it in a parcel to Poland.

Looking through the window, she wondered why there were inexplicable amounts of logs stacked against the fence, when the house had central heating. They were graded according to size, starting off with large logs right down to finely chopped sticks.

After dinner Anton got out the brandy and settled in the armchair. His face shone with the outdoors and his eyes sparkled.

She knew it was time for one of his stories. She loved his tales and spent many hours listening to him. 'I been thinking luff, if you be taking flat, I can be keeping mad cat. He always shitting in my garden anyway! I don't mind him being crazy. He being like Polish cat.'

They had talked about this matter before and Eve now thought the time had come to make a decision. To take up the offer of the flat, or to go and live with Meg. Her sister's boys were both married now and she had the space.

'Maybe he'll be better with you for now. I can take the flat for a while, until I get my money from the sale and: "It won't always be dark at six".' She found herself echoing one of her father's adages.

Anton nodded and then began his story:

'My Grandmother she having crazy cat. She living high in mountains, a good day walking to be getting to her cottage. Walking... walking. I many times be taking things for her. My Mother is baking for all of us - when she could be getting flour and my Grandmother be liking me the best.

She being very old and wrinkling prune.' He laughed. 'Skin like leather and cracking lips kissing me, rough on face. She telling me many stories about kings and queens and gypsies. How we being related to royalty. She reading tea leaves and telling me future. Saying I must be traveling far to get away from Poland...I not believing her one bit!...Well, maybe, sometimes.

Anyway, I loving my Grandmother with all my heart. She looking fierce, but acting soft. One day I visiting with food and parcels, walking for hours until feet hurting like mad. And door being locking luff! I banging on door and shouting her name, but she not answering. So I kicking in door after long time and there she being sitting in rocking chair with cat on face.'

Eve looked puzzled.

'Yes! Luff! CAT SITTING ON FACE! You know what cat be doing luff?'

Eve shook her head, having no idea what he was talking about.

'It eating face! GRANDMOTHER BEING DEAD AND CAT EATING FACE!'

'Oh! My! God!' Eve said in disbelief.

'You know what I be doing next?' he asked, wiping tears from his eyes. 'I KILLING CAT!'

He was silent for a while and Eve didn't say a word. 'So luff! You be taking flat and I be looking after cat?' Eve eyes opened in amazement. 'Don't be worrying luff. I no be killing cat!' he chuckled.

Later on that night she felt a little happier after deciding to take up the offer of the flat. She only hoped it was still available. Opening the music box she took out the second paperweight and admired its unusual design under the light.

Only A Paper Moon

On Eve's Eighth birthday Meg got engaged to Geoff. A May wedding planned. A happy time to look forward to, when the trees were in blossom and bluebells carpeted the ground. During the season when the village folks could escape up to the higher, cleaner woodlands and have picnics. When the daffodils began to curl up, they knew it was time to celebrate. With the sun on their faces, listening to the larks hovering above their heads. No bird calls were heard in the village. The pylons and the smoke kept them away, apart from a few brave sparrows.

Stan and Rose weren't feeling too good. Rose had a painful gum infection and had all her teeth pulled. She had previously told a neighbour, in all seriousness, that she was 'having all her teeth out and a new gas stove put in.' Stan had perfect teeth but decided to join her, just in case. He hated the notion of going for a filling. They were both out for the count for the holidays, until their gums healed. Meg cooked all the Christmas meals. Her parents had Turkey broth.

So Rose agreed Angela should take her younger sister to the Christmas Fair, providing they came home before 9.0.p.m. Angela usually hated dragging her little sister along, but tonight she had an ulterior motive. 'Come on then Evie. Hurry up. Pat will be waiting for me at The Waltzer. So don't get in the way if I get snogged tonight... All right?'

'Close the door. It's getting in my mouth,' their mother wailed.

Both girls laughed at the thought.

They were muffled up against the cold, until they were out of sight from the house. It was a clear smoke free night and their breath steamed out in front of them. The moon, like a waxy white ball painted on a black canvas, managed to push through the grime.

An alien sight to the villagers. Then Angela unwrapped and put on her make-up at the bus shelter, back-combed her hair and took out a pair of pink stiletto heel shoes from her handbag. Instead of looking thirteen years old, she was more like a young woman. She made her transposition into womanhood very early. She was now 'Doris Day' and Eve was a little jealous. 'Aren't they our Meg's shoes?' Eve asked.

'So? If you tell her, you're dead!' Angela chewed on her gum then blew a large pink bubble, popping it in Eve's face.

"If your sweetheart Sends a letter of goodbye..." Johnny Ray blasted out from the fairground ride. Angela made straight for The Waltzer, where Pat waited. The best looking lads always worked there. Spinning the girls round and making them scream. It was also much warmer undercover. Eve looked on as her sister made eyes at the dark- haired man blowing smoke rings out of his pursed lips. He had a mop of black curls and deep set brown eyes, with a wildness that Angela found intriguing.

Eve became bored and searched for Mrs. Pinkerton's stall. She was in the same place as usual. Wearing a bright red satin dress with a matching cape, and a bow with cherries on, in her enormous bouffant hair-do. 'Hello! Flame-haired child,' she called over to the girl. 'Where is the rest of your family?'

'Dad and Mum are poorly. They've had all their teeth out, but keep being sick in the bucket and groaning. Nan and Meg are busy sewing all our bridesmaid dresses.'

'And the Blonde Bombshell is making the goo-goo eyes at wild boy,' Mrs. Pinkerton laughed, looking over at The Waltzer. Angela's screams were heard above the rest. Her pink chiffon petticoats, stiffened with sugar and water, were rising up round her waist. Eve felt embarrassed for her sister.

'Do you want something special for your birthday, or will you ignore an old gypsy's warning again?'

'Yes!.. No! Miss!' said Eve - a little scared.

'Don't fret so child. You're too young to trouble yourself about those older than you,' she said kindly. 'Life is too short for long worrying. 'Here take this for a shilling - and remember - find the meaning and follow the path,' she added, handing her a deep blue paperweight.

'Oh! It's so beautiful. Thank You.' Eve studied the glass dome and saw swirls of white among the blue, like waves in the sea.

Mrs. Pinkerton began to speak again, but stopped herself, not wanting to burden one so young with sad tales of the future. Instead she said, 'Tell your sister over there to beware a man with the initial K! Take this for your mother and tell her "Yield not to temptation for still waters run deep." Can you remember all that? God keep you safe. Stay sheltered until the Blonde Bombshell remembers the time and returns to reality.'

Mrs. Pinkerton lowered her enormous round eyes and brought out some more china and glass from a cardboard box under the stall, then began filling up the empty spaces. Eve said over and over in her head what Mrs. Pinkerton had told her. She looked at the paperweight for her mother and it had a tiny red apple in the middle.

That night Angela made her mind up to marry Keith - and no one, not even a gypsy's warning would stop her, even if she had to run away and join him. They kissed passionately behind the Big Basket, until Angela remembered the last bus left the square at 10.45p.m. The girls didn't get home until 11.30.p.m. Angela had a quiet telling off from her father behind closed doors. Her mother would have given Angela a quick clip round the head, if she'd been quick enough to catch the girl. But their father had a firm way of speaking, which chastened her more than any untimely swipe.

It was impossible to stay mad at Angela for long, even when her parents saw the love-bite on her neck, the next morning. Her zest for life was contagious. Unknown to them, she had written a love letter to Keith. Poured Meg's expensive Chanel No.5 perfume over it. Persuaded her friend Pat to deliver it by hand. She was sworn to secrecy.

'What did you buy with your birthday money Evie?' Meg asked, at the breakfast table.

'I got this from Mrs. Pinkerton and she said that Angela had to beware a "K".'

'We don't know any K's. Do we?' their mother asked, looking at Angela.

'Only Kettleborough's Ice Cream and that's always all right,' replied their father, winking at Eve.

'What a lovely paperweight Evie,' Meg said, holding it up to the light. 'It's like the sea at Yarmouth.' Meg had booked a holiday in Great Yarmouth for her honeymoon. The brochures littered the sofa.

'Why don't we all go?' Eve said, remembering Mrs. Pinkerton's words. She knew her parents needed a break and it would be their first holiday since Skegness. This must be the meaning of the blue paperweight!

'What do think Mags? Would Geoff mind? We wont be going to stay in your posh hotel. More like a caravan holiday.'

'That would be lovely Dad. All of us together!' Meg replied. 'Geoff won't mind one bit!'

Nan rolled her eyes, in the same way that Angela always did. Eve waited for her mother to go into the kitchen to do the washing up. 'This is for you Mum. Mrs. Pinkerton said: "Yield not to temptation for still waters run deep".'

'Chance would be a fine thing!' her mother replied, looking into the paperweight. 'Although your Nan has often said your Dad is "still waters".'

Angela was listening at the door and said, 'Old Nutter!' before flouncing off.

When the Fair left town Angela became very quiet. Locking herself in her bedroom for hours after school. Writing love letters, as many as three a day, hoping at least one would find him in the next town. Meg became suspicious when her Chanel perfume lost its smell and left brown streaks on her neck and wrists. Angela had replaced it with tea.

After further investigation, Meg found Angela's secret daily pile of billet-doux, smothered in perfume. Eve confessed to Meg about the young gypsy man who worked on The Waltzer. Meg enlightened their mother. Rose informed Stan. Then it was forgotten, when no word was heard from him. They were relieved. Angela gradually forgot the handsome gypsy, after she ran out of spending money for writing paper and stamps. "There are plenty more fish in the sea," her father said.

The following October a post card with a picture of Nottingham Goose Fair, dropped through the letter box. Keith intended to meet up with her at Christmas. A whole year between their last encounter.

Angela was told she must never see him again. Forbidden fruit made the rendezvous dangerous and exciting. Her parents didn't realize by banning their liaison Angela became Juliet, aching for her Romeo. With Meg's new bottle of perfume hidden under lock and key, Angela used lavender polish mixed with rose petals instead.

La Mer

It was their first day in Great Yarmouth and the weather stayed fine and dry. Eve's mother pushed an enormous amount of bacon round the pan on the small calor-gas stove, while her father went to fetch the water. The caravan felt cosy and warm, as the gas fire had been on since they'd returned from their mornings ablutions over at the wash house. 'Angela! Stop day dreaming and butter that toast. Evie! Set the table, it's nearly ready... Go and find your Nan, she's bound to be checking out the bingo...Don't dawdle...Have you washed your necks?...Do you want beans or tomatoes with your breakfast?...I've only got four sausages so one of you will have to do without...Do you want fried bread?... Just in time Stan...Who wants tea?' she said as their father returned carrying two pales of water.

The girls giggled at their mother's many questions and both answered differently, flustering her even more. Their voices almost the same. Rose's brilliant white dentures clicked as she talked, making everything twice as funny. Stan developed a piercing whistle on his 'S's.' Despite this, Rose and Stan set a trend. Most of the folks in the village were so impressed with their sparkling dentures, they queued up at the Dentists for full extraction. Free on the NHS.

As the weather gradually warmed up, Eve happily watched her parents and Nan relaxing in the deck-chairs. Sheltered by the sand dunes, they read the paper and drank their tea. The tension dropping slowly from their faces as the warm sun unwound them. Her father took ages hammering in the wind-breaker with a large pebble, then the wind changed. The endless white sand and the seagulls calling overhead. And the air so fresh it made her dizzy.

Her father made a car out of sand and Nan took a photograph of Eve sitting in it, with her box Brownie. Some people had bathing costumes on, but Nan said it wasn't becoming for adults to put themselves on show. Although Stan rolled his trousers up to his knees, while Nan laughed at his white legs.

Angela caused a minor panic by disappearing again for two hours. Now she'd grown bigger and more feisty they weren't too worried. The memories of her last wandering still worried them. She was later found by Meg and Geoff, talking to some fishermen.

'Come on Angela. Mum and Dad have been worried sick about you.'

'But I am going on a boat trip with them, now the tide's in.'

'Oh! No! You're not!' said Meg, dragging her sister away from the ruddy faced men.

'Spoil sport!' they all shouted.

Meg and Geoff held hands and smiled all the time, through lunch, while Angela rolled her eyes in contempt.

'Can I go down to the sea Mum?' Eve asked, later that afternoon. 'I want to collect some shells.'

'All right, but remember to walk in a straight line down that path of dry sand and look for the Life Boat coming back, we're sitting to the right.'

'Do you think that's wise Rose? We don't want you fretting -,' her husband questioned.

'I won't worry Stan. I know you'll be watching her like a hawk.'

'And keep your sun hat and cardie on,' shouted Nan.

She walked bare foot down towards the sea, noticing the worm casts scattered along the damp sand either side of the path, picking up pink and perfect shells on her way.

'Evie Watts? Yoo! Hoo! ...Over here!' A small girl with dark brown hair, waved at her. It was Vera Butterworth in a knitted swimming costume, splashing and squealing in the water with her sister and three brothers. The wetter the costume got, the more it stretched. She didn't care.

'Hello,' Eve said shyly.

'Can you swim?' Ted asked, walking towards her.

'No!'

'Don't you dare Ted Butterworth, or I'm telling Mam,' Vera said scowling at her older brother, who was about to pick Eve up and throw her into the waves. Ted, a tall lad with smiling brown eyes, was generally shy with the opposite sex. Eve was shyer. This gave him confidence. She had a big crush on him, from that day onwards. Donald O'Conner took second place.

'I can swim!' Vivian shouted out, plunging into the water. She was Vera's older sister and could do everything perfectly. Cartwheels, handstands, dancing, singing, impressions, double-back bends. You name it she could do it.

'Come on!' said Vera, moving away from her sister. 'She's showing off again! I'll show you how to swim when Lauren Bacall's shifted.' She remembered Vera from school, but they sat at different ends of the classroom. In a room filled with forty children, it's hard to get to know each other well.

'Do you want an ice-cream cornet?' Vera asked.

'Yes please Vera.'

'Then follow me - and don't call me Vera. That's my Sunday name. I'm just Vee! Although our Charlie calls me Bee, so our Freddie now calls me Beewaspy.' Charlie was her little brother, aged four, who followed her everywhere. Eve wished she had a little brother. From that day he might as well have been, because he followed her around as well.

Vee's mother and father, Jessie and Johnny, were sitting in deck-chairs at the other side of the Life Boat. She noticed the darkness of their skin. They both shone like burnished mahogany, rubbed down with lashings of coconut oil. Unlike her own mother, who, despite using pots of Nivea on her face, was turning decidedly redder by the minute, even with a scarf covering her head. Vee noticed Eve staring at her parents. 'My Dad's from Yarmouth, so we come here every school holiday to stay with our Gran. That's why they look so mucky!'

Her mother laughed and then threw a beach ball at her, saying: 'Cheeky little bugger!'

'Mam! This is Evie Watts from number 23. Can we have an ice-cream cornet?'

'Do you think I'm made of money? Here!' she said, handing over a shilling. 'Now clear off. Go and pester somebody else... Don't forget to take Charlie with you!'

Her mother sat back and closed her eyes, soaking up the sun once more.

'Vee? Why does your mother wear curlers all the time?'

'Not all the time. You see she takes 'em out every Saturday night and puts her teeth in, when they get dolled up to go to the pub. She washes her hair on Sunday night and for the rest of the week she keeps the curlers in, because the curls last longer that way.'

'Oh! I see!' she said, understanding. Vera, her brothers and their mother had thick straight brown hair, whereas Vivian was the only blonde in the family.

'Come on lazy bones. Race you to the ice-cream man!'

'Wait for me Bee and Beebie!' Charlie shouted.

The friendship forged on that day lasted for the rest of their lives, even though they lost touch with each other for years at a time. As did that of the two woman sitting on opposite sides of the Life Boat.

I Love To Boogie

When Eve and Vee first started dancing classes, they were held at the old school in the village. It was a decrepit old building some 200 years old. The hall also sufficed for: Scout meetings, Whist Drives, Film Shows, Concerts, Tombola Night, Youth Club and Sunday School.

Stan taught the youngster how to box and perform gymnastics, and his work mate, Jack Frost, instructed them in Jujitsu. The two men were heroes to the unruly lads who attended, especially when Stan performed the Crucifix on the rings. He'd not done this for a while, but put on a good show, hoping the bolts around the ropes would hold. Rose rubbed him down that night with 'Firey Jack.'

After dance class the children watched a monochrome film show, either: Popeye, The Perils of Pauline, Laurel and Hardy, or The Three Stooges. Most of the time the films snapped, or the projection machine broke down, leaving the kids stamping and whistling in the dark, shouting: 'Put a penny in the slot.'

On Sunday mornings Eve and Vee quite often missed Sunday School lessons and went up to the woods instead. With their penny collection money they bought a half-penny liquorice and a sherbet dip each. It wasn't as if they were disobedient children. Far from it. Scared out of their wits by the preacher, who had two thumbs on his right hand, spouting on about "Leprosy, Stigmata - and Hell Fire and Damnation."

Eve said Jesus was more likely to be found in the woods. And they looked for Him behind every tree and down every rabbit hole. This was confirmed when they both got a Bible each for good attendance.

The dance teacher Miss Maclean, decided they should do a concert, consisting of tap and ballet routines and a story loosely based on 'Snow White.' Naturally Vivian got the lead role after an elaborate performance of back-flips and cartwheels and a very good Al Johnson impression. This decision put Judy Taylor's nose out of joint. She expected to be more than a mere understudy, having had drama and elocution lessons. She also looked the part with her chubby round face and short black hair. On the night of the performance the hall filled. Eve and Vee did two chorus-line tap dancing performances, along with the rest of class. They jigged about to 'Good Morning' and 'Ball in the Jack,' in sequined costumes. Vivian pranced an energetic solo in front of them. Vee pulled faces at her talented sister, behind her back and made everyone laugh. Eve also played Dopey and Vee an unlikely Grumpy.

They also had roles of rabbits in the woods. It was this penultimate woodland scene with Vivian rejoicing in her love, after coughing up the apple, that things began to go wrong. Nearly the whole cast was on stage and danced around, wildy crashing into each other. The bunny-eared, whiskered rabbits hopped, the fairies skipped, the pirates swash-buckled and Vivian twirled madly around the prince. Some of the tiny tots started to cry in the confusion, until Margaret Clarke guided them off the stage. Seven of the rabbit ran off stage for a quick change back into their dwarf costumes. Miss Maclean hammered away undaunted on the piano, as Vivian prepared herself for a tricky six back-flips ending in the splits, across the tiny stage. The final stupendous performance. As she reached the middle, she disappeared from sight with a mighty crash. The rotten stage collapsed under the weight - and panic followed.

Fortunately Vivian only sustained cuts and bruises, much to Vee's delight. She laughed so much her beard fell off. The stage was never repaired owing to lack of funds. All future concerts were relocated to the Church Hall.

☙

Eve opened the music box again, when the phone rang. It was Meg ringing from Florence.

'It's Angela. She was arrested for disorderly conduct and locked up all night!' Meg sounded really fed up.

'What's she done now?'

'You know Angela! She always late and in a tizz and will cause as much fuss as possible if she's annoyed.'

Meg began in her slow soft voice: 'When she and Keith finally picked us up on the way to the airport, they were an hour late. Then we couldn't find a space in the car park and had to walk miles. Eventually we got in the queue for our Pisa flight and Keith had forgotten their passports. He'd left them in the glove compartment, his mind being on 'other things'. So he hot-footed it back to the car park while we queued for the check-in desk.

Well, because their names were on the tickets as the lead party, we couldn't check in for them, not without the passports. By this time we were all fed up, especially when we had to go to the back of the queue.

Poor old Keith was worn out when he got back with the passports and sweating cobs. Angela had packed three suitcases: one full of presents, then there was one fit to bursting with her clothes, and a smaller one for Keith. She had to pay excess baggage. Heaven knows what she'd got in there but they weighed a ton. All the smoking seats were filled. So this made her madder. Then they had to hold the plane up for us. Everyone was furious when we finally boarded. Of course, our poor Angela was dying for a fag. So off she trecked down to the loo with cigs and lighter on show, only to be told to return to her seat as smoking was not allowed in our section of the plane. Then she started an argument with the air hostess, a real snooty cow, according to Angela, and had to be escorted back to her seat by two very nice boys in uniform. I got her a drink to calm her nerves and mine. But one is never enough for her, is it? By the time we landed she was well out of it. Singing Shirley Bassey songs at the top of her voice. Keith sat with Geoff and ignored her all the way.

As you know our Angela never gets much chance to wear all the jewelry that Keith buys her: so she'd put the lot on. Massive diamond rings flashing. Gold necklaces clanging and bracelets galore. You know how she walks, in that kind of cocky jigging way. So she clattered through customs, like the 'Piratess of Penzance', holding the small suitcase belonging to Keith, while he struggled with the heavy bags.

Unbeknown to Keith she'd put 3 pounds of smoky bacon and 5 pounds of kippers in the small suitcase, wrapped in foil inside her Yorkshire pudding tin; right on top of Keith's clothes. Apparently Richard misses these delicacies like mad and can't get them in Florence; especially his Yorkshire Pudding.

By this time she is very uncoordinated and dying for a pee. Impatient as ever she tried to jump the queue at customs control. Jewelry clattering, tottering on four inch heels, buttocks clenched together - and being one for flirting, as you know, she started giving the customs officer the eye. It usually worked for her, but not when she's had a few.

'This way madam please,' he said, beckoning her over. We all follow.

'Anything to declare?' he asked.

'No!' she said, getting more annoyed by the minute and looking guilty as hell.

He saw Keith struggling to lift the suitcase with the Christmas presents, up on the counter and said: 'Open please!'

Angela tried to find the keys and dropped the contents of her bag. Tampax rolled everywhere. If you could have seen Geoff s face, it was a picture. Anyway when she got it open the officer asked her what's inside the presents.

Our Angela's face got redder and redder and her speech more blurred. She said, 'If you think I'm opening this lot, you've another think coming. I didn't finish work until chuffing six o'clock last night and I had to wrap these bloody things up, before I got to bed. We were up this morning at five so don't mess with me love. I'm at that time of the month!'

Then she picked up one large present and shook it. It jingled. 'That's a present for my son's girlfriend, Maria. It a giant rabbit with bells on.' Then she picked up another one and shook it about. 'That's after-shave for my son,' she went on 'and this is a chuffing book that plays music for Maria's baby sister - and this is a blinding photo frame for her mother! And this is a box of bleeding cigars for her dad!' Until she'd been through the whole lot, swearing worse with each present. You know - the 'F' word. The people behind us, who she'd pushed in front of, started to get really mad, so Angela told them to 'Sod off,' putting up two fingers. Then she burst into song. A very silly chorus of: "All I want for Christmas is my two front teeth."

'You can go,' the officer said, not wanting a riot. He chalked a cross on all the cases and waved us on. So, Geoff and I breathed a sigh of relief. Poor Keith tried to find a trolley and couldn't and he's left with the bags again. We managed to get near the exit for a taxi, when a guard appeared with an Alsatian sniffer - dog. Our Angela spotted a 'Ladies' and headed off, trying to dance in time to the piped music. Dean Martin I think it was. She wiggled her backside, carrying the small suitcase, swaying from side to side. Then she burst into "Diamonds are Forever..." The dog in hot pursuit and pulling hard on the lead. You can guess what happened next!

Well, the guard grabbed Angela by the scruff of the neck and pulled her back. She turned round and wacked him, thinking its Keith behind her and peed her pants. The dog went berserk and tried to mount her leg, so she punched the dog. Keith just sat on the suitcases holding his head.

She's being released in a hour. They laughed so much down at the Police Station, when they found the kippers and bacon, she got off with a fine. Of course she bawled her eyes out. Then told them all they looked like Robert de Niro.'

Apparently they thought this outrageous English woman a rare commodity and couldn't believe it when they saw totally unrepressed emotions.

'Trust our Angela to come out smelling of roses...Are you there Evie?' Meg asked.

Eve was on the floor, choking with laughter. The doubled edged joke was that Meg didn't find the escapade funny, so Eve was trying to restrain herself. 'Yes!' she gasped. 'But it's Keith who'll be smelling of kippers!' She decided as the holiday drew to a close, that with such wacky people around her, life wasn't so bad.

Bridge Over Troubled Waters

Stan injured his wrist at work but hadn't told anyone, not even Rose. Gradually it got worse and some of the bone was removed. He was off sick for twelve weeks unable to lift anything. Compensation was ruled out because it hadn't been recorded it in 'The Accident Book'. The rent needed paying and the kids wanted new shoes, in one of the coldest Winter's on record. The only good thing to come out of it was his eczema dried up completely. Both Angela and Eve had to sacrifice their dancing lessons for a while. Stan stopped the athletics training, so the loss of the little money he earned from it, compounded the problem. Meg helped as best she could, but she and Geoff struggled to manage their mortgage.

'There's not much else I can do,' Rose said. 'The money I get from cleaning and ironing from Ma Crowfoot isn't enough,' she told Jessie.

'Look lass. I've heard their taking women on at the factories in Sheffield. Let's go and see if we can get in.'

At that moment Joan Smith knocked on the back door and walked in.

'All right Rose, Jessie....I was wondering whether you could lend us a bucket of coal I'll pay you back at the end of the week.' The forty year old woman had dull grey hair and her eyes were sunk into hollow sockets.

'She's got enough on with her own family to look after!' said Jessie.

'It's all right,' Rose said, gesturing for her friend to be quiet. She walked to the coal house and unlocked the door. Usually it was stacked high with a wooden board to keep it all in, but now Rose had to remove the board to reach the coal at the back.

'Here you are love. It's all I can spare,' she said filling the woman's bucket.

'Hang on a minute lass,' Nan said, going into the pantry. She made a twist of tea and sugar, took a bottle of milk, six scones and a fresh baked loaf and put them all in a brown paper bag.

'All the best Rose. Thanks Mrs. Watts!' the ailing woman said, accepting the food as if it were a feast. 'What on earth's happened to your Angela's face and hair? she added, noticing the girl trying to hide under the quilt. Angela was sitting in the best armchair in her nightie and sporting a black eye and shorn hair.

For some reason the girls' school she attended decided to change the uniforms style. Update it. Instead of gym slips and straw hats, the girls were to wear berets and skirts. Money was tight, so Rose dyed her yellow beret navy blue, leaving it to dry in the oven, stretched over a dinner plate. Meg altered one of her old navy blue skirts to fit Angela. It was bad enough having to wear Meg's old moth eaten blazer, so Angela threw a strop.

'They'll never know the difference,' Rose said, sewing in the name tapes. Angela wasn't happy. She was sick of hand-me-downs - and being the middle child. Meg got new things, and Angela's second hand clothes were always worn out by the time it came to Eve's turn.

No one noticed anything different, until that awful day in poured down with rain on her way home from school. The other kids laughed at her and she didn't know why until she got home. When she took off the beret she had a deep blue line across her forehead and a stripe of dye running down the back of her neck. The tops of her ears were navy blue, but worst of all, her lovely blonde curls were a brilliant shade of air-force blue. Angela screamed and bawled. Meg and her mother couldn't help but laugh. 'Don't worry love. It'll wash out...Come here,' her mother said, still chuckling.

After scrubbing and rubbing with carbolic soap Angela's face and neck were red raw - and still stained. Her mother then started to scrub her hair until her scalp burned. 'Will you keep still...What am I to do? It looks as if I shall have to cut the at least six inches off. That's where most of the dye's seeped in.'

Now if there's one thing which sent Angela ballistic, it was any reference to hair and scissors. Before her mother could rinse away the third lot of suds, she ran straight out of the scullery and into the flat edge of the open door. Bump then silence. Angela was on the floor and moaning softly. Her left eye already starting to close. 'Heaven help us,' shouted Rose. 'Stan what's to do? Can you help me?'

Stan leaped up and got a cold compress for her eye, then carried her into the kitchen. 'That's no good. Get that rump steak I bought for your tea. Slap in on quick!'

'I don't want a dead cow on my face!' she bawled.

'You'll do as you're told lady!...Whatever are the neighbours going to think? It's no good, she'll have to stop off school,' Rose said.

Angela stopped crying and peered from under the steak, asking: 'Can I have a pillow and an eiderdown, and lie in the best armchair in front of the fire, in my nightie? ...I won't tell anybody what you did to me mum,' she said, knowing how to wind up Rose. 'And can I have that big box of chocolates in Mrs. Pound's window, you know the one with the cottage picture on?'

Rose was just about to shout at her, when Stan burst out laughing. 'I don't see why not Angela. As long as you let me have the ones with nuts in!'

'And can I have some of your steak, with chips instead of sausage for my tea?' she asked her dad cheekily, waving the raw meat around.

Angela's air-force blue locks were shorn off, leaving her with a little halo of lamb's tails. She hated it. Everyone else said how much she looked like her name: an angel. It was after a full week off school, that someone suggested white spirit to remove the stains on her face. Rose found an old bottle of turpentine on the cold slab at the back of the pantry. It did the trick.

It was at this time when Angela accidently knocked her mother's prized bone-china figure off the mantle-piece. Eve did her homework while she watched children's television. Angela admired herself in the mirror, after Carol Moxon had said she looked like Kim Novak with her new hairstyle. Her eye was now a bright shade of yellow and her hair had a silver hue.

Eve heard the clatter, then saw the cause. They both knew their mother would go ballistic. The figure of an Edwardian lady with spaniel dog was a family heirloom.

'Is there any of Dad's glue left in the outhouse?' Eve suggested in panic.

They couldn't find anything to stick the head back onto the body. Then Angela had an idea.

'Chewing gum!' she said, sighing with relief. She stuck the head back onto the figure and trimmed the excess gum. 'She won't notice...Will she?'

'No.'

That night as Rose and Stan watched 'What's My Line?' on the new 9" Ultra T.V. in the front room, something strange happened. The chewing gum began to melt from the heat of the fire. The head rolled slowly to one side, then dangled for a while before it dropped gently onto the mantle-piece. Chewing gum still attached to the body.

This was the only time the girls had their backsides tanned by their mother. Not for breaking the ornament, but for not owning up. Eve took her punishment along with Angela, despite being innocent. The sisters cried themselves to sleep, holding on to each other.

After Joan Smith left, clutching her bag of goodies, that same afternoon it took Rose and Jessie an hour's walk in the freezing cold, before they reached the grimy steel works at Brightside. The road that ran parallel was called Sunnyside. Whoever named these places had a wry sense of humour. To their surprise it was even more grim than the village. The factory walls there were so high they couldn't see daylight.

'So you think yer can do a man's job lasses?' the foreman asked, amid the clatter. 'Yer don't look very strong, especially "Ginger Rogers" there.'

'Course we can mester,' Jessie intervened. 'I've reared five kids and buried three, so don't tell me about being the weaker sex.'

He stopped smiling. 'Well, I'll give yer a tryout. Ten shillings a week, basic and if yer does piece-work yer can earn a bob or two extra. Righto?' he smiled at Rose adding, 'Remember to wear a turban to keep yer 'air out o't'way o't'machines.'

Rose and Jessie had to get up a four in the morning, so they paid Albert Goody, 'The Knocker-upper' to wake them. He never slept and did no end of jobs, including rat-catching. As knocker-upper he could earn two pence a day from each house, tapping on the bedroom window with a long pole, making sure they weren't late for work.

He was totally reliable and never failed them. On fishing trip days he had to get the men up a 3 a.m. so they paid him a penny extra and in exchange he provided them with a bucket of maggots, hand-reared in the bodies of dead rats.

One particularly cold morning Jessie wasn't feeling so good, so Rose had to do the long walk on her own. She was exhausted and had lost a lot of weight. Her boots were letting in water causing the blister on her chilblains to burst, but she carried on until she reached the canal bank, breathing heavily.

A thick mist hung over the water that morning, as if to hide the indiscretions floating on its surface. All the slimy waste left over had been vomited out into the canal, but didn't show up in the twilight. At this ungodly hour Rose thought the canal had a strange alluring beauty about it. The surface looked like rippled silk. She walked to the edge and stood for a while, staring down into the darkness. Her hands were freezing and raw so she put them into her pockets, feeling for the hot potatoes. Nan had slipped one into each pocket to keep her warm and she could eat them for breakfast later. It didn't really matter because she had come to the end of her resolve. One faltering step forward would have been enough to thrown her into the blackness. If the coldness didn't kill her than the pollution would.

It was at that moment, the choice between living and dying, that Rose thought about her children. The words: "Still waters...," drifted into her head. How could she leave them, but she wanted to go so badly - to escape. It was too hard to stay, living took too much out of her and left her with nothing of herself.

'Hold on Rose,' shouted Jessie. 'Just made it lass. Had to drag myself out of bed, I did.'

As Jessie linked arms with Rose in the darkness, pulling her away from the edge, not a word was spoken. Walking along the tow-path Jessie said cheerily, 'Come on, hurry up lass. It's too bloody cold to be loitering round here.'

'Jessie?'

'Aye lass?'

'Do you ever think of, well you know -'

'Many a time love. But the thought of the babbies always stops me.' Rose started to cry. 'Now then lass. Come on let's show them buggers how we women can sling them bars and do twice as much work for half as much money - and still look bloody beautiful!' she laughed, patting her curlers.

The sound of rough masculine voices, good-naturedly swearing over a joke, spurred them forward. Hurrying into the warmth of the factory, the two women steeled themselves for the hard labour ahead.

Don't Look Back In Anger

It was the last day at school before the Christmas Holidays. Vee and Eve were busy painting Christmas cards for their mothers, when the Head Master brought in a new boy. The whole class jumped to its feet, banging the wooden seats up behind them. All of them were feeling nervous by this unexpected visit.

'Good afternoon Mr. Barker,' they all sang out.

'Good afternoon children. This is Peter Hill and he will join you in the New Year.' The boy looked around at the unsmiling faces and shuffled nervously on the spot. 'Stand to attention boy and don't move!' Mr. Barker ordered.

The school was run like a military operation. Mr. Barker had served in the war and it had mentally scarred him. Children as young as four were made to march into assembly as he called out 'Quick march! Left Right! Left Right! Halt! About face! Stand at ease!' They were not allowed to sit down all through prayers. Many a child fainted through the ordeal. No one would dare to help them, so they were left until assembly had finished; or they got to their feet again.

When Rose's girls started school, they all stayed for school dinners. The dinner ladies were kind and generous and always gave the kids extra helpings. Good home-cooking of substantial two course meals. The Granger's, a family of seven children often returned for third helpings. Mr. Marsh and Miss Johnson supervised the operation, making sure each child had a good meal inside them.

For some reason Mr. Barker decided on a dinner inspection. He usually had his meal in his room. He walk behind the children as they were eating, making sure they sat up straight and clearing their plates. The smell of cabbage, sour milk and sweet custard filled the air, along with stink of unwashed children. Teachers got used to it. Left-handed Angela caught the attention of the Head Master.

'Eat with you knife in your right hand child... NOW!' Angela swapped her cutlery round and tried to cut the tough meat. She succeeded in flipping it across the table, splashing the gravy everywhere. The domineering man's face turned from purple to red. He reminded Eve of a bull-dog about to bite, until she noticed Angela crying her eyes out. It was the first time Eve had seen the Head Master's face soften. He cleared his throat and said: 'Make sure you practice at home girl,' before walking over to another table.

Angela refused to stay for school dinners again. She was terrified of the man, who on that same afternoon did a classroom inspection. He decided to take the lesson and forced six year old children to do joined up italic writing, with straight nib, pen and ink. They'd not done this before. Miss Johnson was terrified and thought herself a failure, until Vee and Eve brought her a paper daisy chain they'd made.

Her sister came home from school in a wild mood, her fingers covered in ink. She tried really hard to write with her right hand that evening. The same night she sneaked out and threw a brick through grumpy old Mrs. Thompson's backdoor window. Afterwards she whistled all the time. Had a D.A. or 'Duck's Arse' short hair cut, and went through a tomboy stage for six months. She was glad Mr. Barker didn't take classes again. He retired shortly after Christmas, blubbering in front of the whole school when the Deputy Head presented him with a barometer.

At this moment it was Peter Hill's turn to be scared out of his wits by the Cane-Lashing-Square-Bashing Sargeant Major. The boy's most lasting memory of his first afternoon at the new school though, was of Vee and Eve giggling at his discomfort. He was left in Mr. Marsh's care to join the painting class. He sat at the same table as the girls.

Both boys and girls liked Mr. Marsh. The girls all fancied him and the boys wanted to be in his class, because he never sent them to the Head Master for a caning. Instead he took them into the stockroom behind the blackboard and thwacked their backsides with his plimsole. Poor Reggie Slater got more than his fair share of beatings. He tried his best, but Dyslexia wasn't recognized in those days. He was pigeonholed as lazy and that was the end of it. Out of all the village kids Reggie was the most successful when he left school at fifteen.

The Council workmen disconnected all the copper boilers as they were condemned as unsafe. At that time enterprising Reggie worked as a ragman's assistant. Over a period of weeks, he collected around five hundred boilers on the cart. He made a fortune selling them on for scrap. Folks were glad to be rid of them and he made 100% profit. A balloon cost nothing. The rag-man was too old to care and Reggie became a Scrap Metal Merchant, exchanging the horse for a truck.

He married Frieda Allcock. The poor, round-shouldered girl with nits and a purple tongue, half shaved head, ring-worm and impetigo. Special swimming lessons in Sheffield were arranged to improve her posture. The scruffy, raggy-arsed kid turned into the best dressed lad in the village and was the first to buy his own house. Frieda became quite the elegant lady. 'You reap what you sow,' Stan remarked.

'Where you from then?' Vee asked the shy new boy, cheekily.

'Lincolnshire,' he replied, looking at the girl with the flame-coloured hair.

'Where's that when its at home?' Vee quizzed him.

'Skegness!'

'Skeggie! "It's Very Brasing",' Vee laughed. 'Don't you talk posh?'

'Leave him alone,' Eve said. 'I'm Evie and the one with the mouth is Vee. Do you want to share our paints?' From that moment Peter Hill, or "Peetrill" as Vee called him, was smitten with the green eyed girl.

On Eve's Ninth birthday, Peter, Vee and Ted were allowed to go the fair on their own. The sound of Alma Cogan's record blaring out: "Sugar-time," from The Caterpillar, in her catchy giggling way, clashed like mad with Guy Mitchell's energetic version of: "She wears Red Feathers and a Hula-Hula Skirt," resounding from The Bumping Cars. Vee, Ted and Peter went on The Dive Bomber, while Eve tried to find Mrs. Pinkerton.

She walked there alone, because she knew Vee would be cheeky. Also she didn't want her best friend cursed. Mrs. Pinkerton sat there as always, well maybe a little larger, Eve thought. She wore an orange and yellow dress, which looked more like a tent. She had orange plastic dice earring and matching bright orange lipstick. Eve noticed her circles of rouge were also orange, but the rest was unchanged. The hair just sat there like a huge black candy floss above the arched eye-brows.

'Hello there flame-haired girl. How you have grown!'

'Hello Mrs.Pinkerton. Mum says: "Thank you for the advice and the paperweight..." And Nan sent you these,' Eve added, giving the woman a bag full of baking.

'Rock buns and tea cakes - delicious. Thank your mother and your Nan for me.'

'Can I buy another paperweight please?'

'I thought you'd never ask child!' she said reaching under the counter. 'One shilling only, special offer.'

Eve took the paperweight and waited for the warning, but none came.

'Shall I look into it, like this,' Eve said holding the paperweight up to her eye.

'Only if you want child. Life goes on! Now go find the boy with the bright blue eyes and slow smile - and have fun!'

Mrs. Pinkerton was acting funny Eve thought. Not like her usual mysterious self.

Still the paperweight was lovely with a circle white lilies in the centre. She popped it into her shoulder bag and ran to find her friends.

Peter and Ted were over at the Coconut Shy and were both aiming at the same coconut, while Vee was concentrating like mad, trying to hook a plastic duck from out of the water, hoping to win a goldfish. She did. It floated on its back, by the time she'd got home.

'I bet "Gypsy Rose Lee" told you to watch out for a tall dark handsome stranger,' Vee said cheekily. 'If so she's right. I've just seen "Six foot and a Gas Lamp" over there with his girl friend.'

Vee, of course, meant their handsome teacher, Mr. Marsh.

Eve was more interested in Peter, noticing his vivid blue eyes, like cornflowers - and he did have a slow smile. It started off with a slight tilting at the corners of his mouth, then moved out to show a dimple on his right cheek, and as it progressed it made his nose crinkle up.

☙❧

28thDecember.

In the empty bedroom, far away from Heathcliffe, all was quiet outside. Most of the neighbours' cars were parked on the drives, windows frosted over. Everyone rested exhausted from burn out after Christmas gluttony, gathering strength for the next onslaught. She thanked heaven Ma Winters was away, having some respite from Gracie Fields singing on full volume, resounding through the walls. Usually she joined in, hair-brush at the ready, with the happy notes of: "Sallyee," but at the moment she needed a little quiet time.

She carefully put the fourth paperweight back into the music box, released the catch and listened to the music, feeling a lump in her throat. Nan had died in the New Year of a heart attack. She went suddenly and left them all in shock. They had forgotten Nan had grown old, that it was her time - and things wear out.

And We'll All Have Figgie Pudding.

The only unhappy memories of Christmas were the times spent at her Grandma Jones's house. Even though there was always chatter and laughter on such occasions she remembered the stories her mother had told of sad past Christmas events within the household. Undertones of ominous happenings always pervaded the festivities. And after a hearty meal and plenty of port and sherry, Eve knew her older aunts and uncles would recollected these occurrences. Christmas was always a time to retell the "Geese Story."

Her Grandma Jones was of Scottish descent, and the family of predominantly redheads, by nature was spirited. They were either elated or depressed, and there was no in-between. Grandma Jones had twelve children and "reared eleven." Baby Ronnie had died of pneumonia one bitterly cold Christmas, while her husband was fighting for his country during The First World War. She had little money to spare, with three other mouths to feed at that time. So while her girls slept, she worked nights, doing everything and anything respectably possible to pay for the funeral. She didn't want her only son to have a pauper's grave. The three girls, all under the age of six, were locked in the house and the key left with the next door neighbour. They were instructed to bang on the adjoining wall if they needed anything.

Rose told Eve how she and her sisters, on the day of the funeral, were dressed in white smocks with black sashes, ribbons and black patent shoes. The glass windowed carriage was drawn by four black horses with feathered plumes. The whole street turned out to watch the tiny coffin, covered in white and red carnations, pass by. Her mother, too distraught to walk, was supported by the other women who had gone through the same tragedy. And it was because of this tragedy that the family didn't celebrate Christmas during their early childhood. It was always a time to remember poor little Ronnie. A time for mourning and reflection on what might have been.

When their father returned from the war, sporting a large curling waxed moustache, things changed. They didn't recognize the tall handsome man in his cavalry uniform and were shy with him for a few days. He soon won them round with tales of battles and blood and gore. His horse was shot from under him by a cannon ball, which blew the beast to smithereens. He showed them bits of shrapnel embedded under his skin, like jagged tattoos. His bayonet hung above the mantle-piece, was kept sharp and shiny, just in case.

Reminders of the horrors he'd seen. He retold tales of murder, mustard gas and massacre, much to the delight of the local children. Acting out and reliving his experiences over and over. Terrifying them with tales of "The Devilish Hun." It was ironic then, that he was the optimistic one. It was fortunate for the family that he had brought some sense of fun back with him, being happy to be alive and well.

Soon their mother became pregnant again, and again. And over nearly as many years, had six sons before she gave birth to another girl. It seemed to be nature's way of balancing things out. Compensating for the loss of millions of men's lives, by producing a surge of post-war baby boys. In a house full of children, her fun-loving husband ensured that Christmas celebrations would not be denied.

'Elizabeth lass. It's time to stop weeping over the loss of one child, when there's the living to tend to,' Joseph said to his wife. 'The bairns need some comfort. Something to be joyful about. Let us thank the Lord that I have work in The Pit, and that our little ones have bread in their bellies and shoes on their feet. We have a warm fire and some coal to spare for others. Things are hard enough for everybody, without being miserable at Christmas. So what do you say? Eh? Come on speak to me.'

'I don't know Jo. It seems disrespectful to our little Ronnie's memory. Don't you think so?'

'Look lass. We've only one life. Time's running forward…Why don't we have a hour at his graveside. Just you and me, to grieve for the little fella. Then we can trim up the house and give the kids a treat.'

'But there's no money to spare. We can't afford a goose, or a chicken even.'

'Leave that to me. We shall have such a good time...Will you play the organ for me again? Make merry and dance? Like you used to? My pretty lass.'

'I'll think about it Jo.'

In the end her husband won her round. She was so glad to have him home and in good spirits. The house was trimmed up with streamers and paper snowflakes stuck on the windows. The Christmas tree was decked with glass feathered birds, ribbons and candles. And an angel with real hair was placed on the top. Each child busied making paper chains from coloured paper and glue. Everyone was happy.

Joseph had made each child a toy carved from the wood of fallen oak branches. They all had a shining new penny, an apple and nuts in their stockings on Christmas morning. Anticipating the delicious feast ahead, the children stood round the set table with its pristine white cloth and best cutlery and crockery, waiting for the meal to be presented. It has been specially cooked by their father. He hadn't allowed his wife into the kitchen and so she played with gusto, Christmas Carols on the organ. Squeezing the bellows between her knees and rolling from side to side in an animated performance that carried on the air to five doors away.

'Come and get it,' shouted their father. 'Dinner's ready.'

All the children clattered to their seats prepared for the meal, knives and forks at the ready. The tureens filled with Brussels sprouts and carrots came first. Then the parsnips and roast potatoes. Enormous squares of Yorkshire Pudding were next. Followed by the brimming gravy boat, and a dish of sausages and apple sauce.

'Where's the chicken dad?' young Iris asked.

'Coming love. It's coming.'

He returned to the kitchen and held up aloft the huge ancient serving dish on which were two small but succulent steaming geese, surround with onion rings and crispy stuffing balls.

Where did you buy them from Jo?' Elizabeth asked.

'Does it matter lass? Let's tuck in. Come on it'll get cold.' He began to expertly carve one of the geese, when his wife rose from her chair and went into the kitchen. A gush of cold air swept into the warm living room as she opened the back door. None of the children dared to start their meal until their parents were seated, so they waited impatiently for mother to return. Then they heard a wail and a sob.

'You've killed them...you murderer. Our Ducky and Quacky,' his wife shouted, running back into the warmth. 'How could you,' she added, her eyes filled with tears.

'Well that's what I got them for in the first place. I've enough mouths to feed without having pets. Especially pet geese for goodness sake.'

At first the children didn't understand. They were too busy concentrating on the feast set in front of them. Then there would be figgie pudding with a silver thrupenny bit for the lucky one. When it finally dawned on them that their pet ducks had been slaughtered by their heroic father, pandemonium ensued. Six children weeping and screaming, with the baby joining in, ruined Joseph's Christmas. They didn't care. He had ruined theirs. Elizabeth refused to eat any of the goose slices offered her. The children did the same. So Joseph: "the murderer" had his meal in silence, apart from his sniffling wife and children, who made do with vegetables and Yorkshire pudding.

He was never forgiven by his wife, for that one act of thoughtlessness, or by the children who were present on that day. Rose still remembered with sadness her only pets. The two fluffy half grown geese, swimming happily around in circles, inside a rubber tyre that had been sliced in half and filled with water. They had answered to their names and followed the children around the garden.

As the years rolled by each Christmas, poor Joseph was reminded of his "cowardly act" by his berating children. After forty years in the coal mines he lost his optimism. So he became sullen and despondent. In retirement, he slept all the time, nodding off in front of the fire, despite the noise of sons and daughters, and grandchildren around him. The older he got the more tetchy he became. He hated Christmas and refused outright to join in the merriment. Grumbling and complaining about how: "Children should be seen and not heard." The fun and games he had as a young man, with his children, were not reserved for his grandchildren.

Eve remembered grumpy granddad Jones, as a roumy eyed old grouch, who never spoke a nice word to her or her cousins. His favourite daughter, gentle Iris, was the only one he confided in, but even her children were ignored. Cousin David, sick of being told off, bought some itching powder and sprinkled it on his granddad's bald head, while he slept. How they laughed as the tormented old man repeatedly scratched his head and nodded off again. As the practical joker of the family David also got some soap that had black ink injected into the hollow centre. He warned grandma not to use it as he had specially bought it for granddad. Their grandmother joined in the joke and didn't let on, forever remembering the unfortunate "murdered" ducks.

It's Too Darned Hot.

It was one of those sweltering hot summer days where it was cooler indoors. 'You can fry an egg on the pavement,' Rose sighed. She and Stan huffed and moaned in the heat. They drank lemonade, laced with sprigs of fresh mint picked from the corner patch, to cool themselves down.

Outside Jude Stonehouse called out: 'Anyee oowd raaag.' Zeus, the old shire horse panted heavily from the weight of the harness and the heat. The ragman gave the beast water to drink, then wiped his neck with a grimy hankie. Rubbing his aching leg, shattered by a land mine during the First World War, he climbed back awkwardly into the cart. The hot weather always made his leg swell and become more painful. He knew it was time to return home. There would be no pickings today. Usually the children ran out in flocks to get their balloons, and to listen to one of his "tall" stories, but now the tar-melted streets were abandoned.

The heat seemed to hang in the valley, as if compressed by the ghastly layer of pollution. And showing through the grime were sections of brilliant china blue sky, dotted with black flecks of dust emitting from the factory chimneys. Milk curdled. Cheese melted. Meat on the cold slab stank and had to be thrown away. Bacon; fly-blown, was slung into the bins. Rose hated waste but there was nothing she could do to avoid it. Usually a bucket of cold water kept the milk cool. Now even the tap water was warm.

Vee and Peter called for Eve. As usual, they had little Charlie in tow, who whizzed around with arms outstretched, totally unaffected by the heat. 'Look at me Evie. I'm in my Spitfire,' he exclaimed.

'We're going to have a picnic in our tent. Are you coming?' Vee asked, giving Eve a knowing look.

'Yes...Mum can I have some food for a picnic in Vee's garden?'

'Don't see why not. Don't go running about and getting heat stroke. Stay undercover and keep your hat and cardie on.'

Stan sighed again. He was on the afternoon shift. The heat in the factory would have built up to unbearable proportions. The men had to work on, regardless, dehydrated and dripping with sweat. He cut up his corned beef sandwiches and put his "mashing" into a two-sided tin. Tea in one end, sugar in the other. A large peeled onion for him and his mate, to be eaten raw with the sandwiches at "Snap Time." Two home-baked tea cakes for afters.

'At least the butter spreads,' he said, dreading the long day's work ahead. 'Shall I make you some corned beef sandwiches Evie?'

Eve nodded. 'Please dad.'

'Fill up those empty pop bottle with water. We don't want you dying of thirst,' her mother instructed. 'And don't forget to bring them back. There's a penny for each one.'

The four friends set off for the picnic. Unbeknown to their parents they intended to have their sandwiches in the extensive woods behind the factories. All the while their mothers believed their children to be safe in each other's back gardens. The friends walked through the old village and made for a short cut down the path behind the pub, alongside the smelting forge. Quickly they ran along the narrow cart track, avoiding brambles, the prickly hawthorn hedges and deadly nightshade growing there in abundance, until they reached the railway lines.

'This is where our Meg's boyfriend got killed. A train hit him you know. Sliced his head clean off,' Eve told Peter. He looked alarmed.

'What shall we do?' Vee asked. 'It's such a long walk round the other way.'

'Stop. Look. Listen,' Peter said warily, echoing the Road Safety instructions.

They stood and listened. Only the sounds of the gigantic relentless lump hammer thudding out, a clattering of steel bars thrown onto the factory floor, and their own nervous breathing, rose above the heat. Flames erupted within the furnaces and white sparks from the hot metal flew around like uncontrolled fireworks.

'I say we go on: Three,' Vee said, feeling scared. 'Come on

Charlie. Don't be worried.' Charlie gave his engine full throttle and pulled up on the joy stick. Holding hands they counted, then flew as if demons from hell were chasing them over the rickety wooden crossing. 'Phew! We made it,' Vee said, laughing with relief.

It wasn't the first time they'd been on the Sheffield side of the valley. Usually they took the long route with their parents, walking under the safety of the railway bridge to get to the lower section of the extensive woods. Today was time for an adventure and a way to find some fresher air. A place where the skylarks sang and the kestrels soared, spreading their wings and gliding in the warm air pockets. It was also a means for the children to escape the oppressive heat, far away from the acrid smell of graphite fumes. They hurried past the bilge tanks and over the wooden railway bridge. A safer way to cross the second busier main-line.

The heavy glass pop bottles weighed them down. 'Let's drink the water. Then we can get some money back on the empties at the shop in Highbank,' Peter suggested.

'I'm tired and hot Bee,' Charlie moaned. 'You carry my pop bottle. Pleeease... It's making my flight path wobbly.'

'Not likely. I feel like a pack horse as it is. Our mam's sandwiches weigh a ton.'

'Give it to me,' Peter offered. 'We'll soon be there. They say it's cooler at the top of the woods. If we make it that far, there should be a nice breeze.'

On their journey the children drained down three bottles of water. Then they split up into sexes and hid behind bushes to take quick pees. The iron-monger's shop in Highbank sold ice lollies and home made toffee apples, as well as nearly every metal appliance known to mankind.

We shall have to drink some more water, if we're to get four penny lollies,' Eve said. They slowly emptied the fourth bottle, not daring to waste the water. The big reservoir in Derbyshire had severely dried out, showing the sunken church's steeple for the first time in years.

'Come on Charlie finish it off. You need to put more petrol in your engine if, you're too fly over the tree tops,' Vee encouraged.

Their little stomach's were filled with sloshing water, as they entered the shop, which was piled high with clanging metal objects. Clutching the bottles, they avoided the rakes, hoes, sheers and spades, kettles, mangles, watering cans and boxes of: nuts, bolts, nails and screws. Weaving in and out of saucepans, dolly tubs, rubbing boards, tin baths and sweeping brushes, they finally reached the counter. The fruity ices, handed over in exchange for the bottles, melted quickly, leaving hands and arms sticky.

Breathlessly they reached the fringe of the woods and surveyed the village below, far away in the distance. Looking down in wonder at their dot-sized homes, nestling beneath a halo of black fumes, the children felt like air-born cherubs up in the cloudless blue sky. And being higher than the two smoking factory chimneys made them feel empowered, and reinvigorated by the pure ether. Charlie revved his engine and prepared for a soft landing.

'I say we eat our sandwiches now,' Vee said, sitting down on a fallen log and wiping sweat from her forehead.

Vee and Charlie had thick jam sandwiches with no butter. Peter had potted salmon paste, cut into triangles and wrapped in grease-proof paper. So they all shared and swapped with Eve. Corned-beef "door-step" sandwiches came out favourite and were classed as the better deal. Stan had put into the bag four Penguin bars. Now all melted. They tasted delicious in spite of the runny chocolate.

'Right,' declared Peter. 'Our adventure starts here! We've got to search for the place where nobody's dared to go for years. Even grownups...Into the depths of the upper woods to find the mysterious: "Dragon's Cave." O.K?'

'But it's supposed to be haunted,' Vee said. 'I'm not going there. Don't want to see ghosts. Do we Charlie?' Charlie nodded and smiled mischievously. He really wanted to see the dragon, so he could shoot it down from his cockpit. 'What about you Evie?'

'Might as well explore while we're here. It's not true anyway. There's no such place...It's just pretend, make believe, to scare us kids away.'

They walked deeper and higher into the middle woods, until the fierce sun was blocked out by a heavy covering of densely packed foliage. Only a small amount of dappled light filtered through. A few lazy bees droned about in confusion, attracted to the children's sticky fingers, while glistening dragonflies danced in and out of uncurling filigree ferns. Columbine and heartsease, feverfew and clover grew in profusion, with nettles - and dock leaves nearby to counteract the stinging rashes on vulnerable bare legs.

'Old Jude told me to look out for some rusted iron railings,' Peter informed them.

After an hour's lengthy trek through bracken and brambles their courage wavered. Deciding upon a few minutes rest to finish off the remainder of Peter's jelly babies, they prepared to move onwards into the undergrowth.

'I think we're lost,' Eve wavered. Then she pointed towards an object in the distance, unable to speak.

'I don't like it. I want to go back,' Vee said, when she saw the twisted railings sticking out of the top of a rocky ridge. It was covered in ivy and overgrown with weeds. A dead tree, with roots exposed, and two crooked arm-like branches, balanced precariously on the edge. It looked as if there had been an earthquake. The land had sliced and fallen away, showing a layer of sand-stone and cracked clay.

'It really exists! Jude swore he was telling the truth,' Peter exclaimed.

'See, there's the entrance. A cave mouth underneath,' Charlie said. We can't stop now Bee. Come on,' he urged, pulling her by the hand. We have to bale out. May Day! May Day! ' he chanted.

'Don't be scared. I've brought my torch. Just in case,' Peter said, tugging on the tangled ivy to make an entrance.

'It's all wet and slimy inside,' Eve protested, as the dampness dripped onto her sun-hat.

'But it's lovely and cool,' Peter said. "Cool," his voice echoed.

Wow!' Vee said. "Wow!"

'HELLO!' Charlie shouted. "HELLO!"

'When I'm calling youooo...' Peter sang. "Youooo," replied.

'Come on let's go further in. It's so nice and cold,' Charlie encouraged his sister.

'But it stinks like dead ferrets,' she said. Not that she'd ever smelled a dead ferret. She deduced that as they stank when they were alive, they must be pretty bad when they're dead.

'Careful! It's quite slippery down here,' Peter said, descending into the darkness.

'Wait for us,' Charlie shouted, following the torch beam.

Vee took hold of Eve's hand and said: 'Don't leave me. Will you?'

'Course not,' she replied, holding on to her friend.

They carefully descended down a narrow passageway into an anti-chamber. An indentation, shaped like a basin, was filled with clear filtered water.

'It looks really deep in the middle. Don't worry. I've got my "Life Saving Badge." Come on lets have a swim,' Peter said, stripping down to his underpants. He put the torch by the side of the water, using its dim circle of light to find his way.

Charlie followed in his Lancaster Bomber, leaping into the middle like a little frog, and making a huge splash. 'Bouncing bombs! Budiong! Budiong!' he shouted. "Budiong!" came back.

'I'm not going in,' Vee said. 'There might be snakes in it.'

'There aren't any snakes in this country. Only adders and they don't have gills,' Peter teased her. 'Come on in scaredy-pants. It's lovely and cold.'

Both girls shyly took off their sandals, socks, hats and cardigans, but left their tops and shorts on. Then they waded into the basin. To Eve surprise it suddenly dropped down and she got a mouthful of cold water. 'It tastes delicious,' she said, gargling and spouting in out, then floated on her back. Her body now wonderfully cool, away from the relentless sun.

Vee swam towards her and doggy-paddled in the middle of the basin.

'No splashing Charlie!' she ordered. "Charlie!"

'O.K.' he said, then began to do scissors kicks with his legs.

'If it's a fight you want - take that,' Vee laughed, pushing a huge wave of water is his direction.

Their screams of laughter echoing around the cave were suddenly silenced by a loud rumbling.

What was that?' Vee asked, shivering.

'I don't know...be quiet,' Peter answered. Then a brilliant flash of light illuminated the cave.

'It's the ghost of the dragon,' Vee wailed. Hurrying to get out of the water, she slipped on the uneven slimy ground and cut her hand as she fell.

The rest of them swam to the edge and huddled together, dripping water everywhere. 'Quick. Dry yourselves on our cardies. Then we'll get out of here,' Eve urged, seeing her friend's distress. She half believed the dragon had come to eat them, for disturbing its rest. 'Here tie my hankie round your hand,' she said taking the wet offering from her pocket.

By this time the torch batteries began to flicker, as they fumbled around in the dimness, trying to get dressed. Another loud rumble and a crack of lightening lit up the cave once more.

'It's only a thunder storm,' Peter said, relieved. 'For a minute I really though it was the dragon and it had got wind of Vee's blood... Whoooo,' he shouted. "Whoooo," came the reply. He carefully climbed back up the narrow passageway, feeling his way along the walls. 'Come on and have a look. It's fantastic.'

'Shut up Peter. You're scaring her more,' Eve chided.

'We're on top of Mount Everest, like Sir Edmund Hilary!' he shouted, ignoring her rebuke and stretching out his arms in triumph. 'See. I can touch the clouds.'

The three of them quickly followed him, peering out through the cave mouth. The sky now pitch black, with anvil shaped clouds looming overhead. A fork of jagged lightning found its mark on one of the ancient trees some fifty yards away. The ground shook and sulphurous burning smells filled the air. The noise deafened.

'Go back inside and keep down,' Peter instructed, instantly becoming mortal again. Knowing they were dangerously unprotected in their wet clothes.

'I think we should get away from here,' Vee said, through chattering teeth. 'I feel something bad is going to happen. This place is haunted. I know it. The dragon's mad at us and it'll be my blood he's after.' Her voice wavered.

'I think she's right,' Eve agreed, shivering. 'It's not safe with all this water dripping around.'

'Where shall we hide then?' Peter asked, looking for a suitable place outside. 'It's wet everywhere now.'

'Anywhere but here,' Vee wailed. 'Come on Charlie. Let's go.'

Charlie entered his cockpit and let off a round of machine gun fire. 'Ack. Ack. Ack. Dragon a twelve o'clock,' he bawled.

The four of them ran out into the woods, as fast as they could. Their feet slipping about in the wet sandals. Away they ran from the cave and headed down to the middle trees. Within seconds the lightning struck the railings on top of the ridge. Then it penetrated down through the ground, finding its way back up from the sandstone in a powerful cyclic motion. Fire and water fused, scorching the earth. The dead tree and foliage on top of the ridge, were burned black and frazzled to a cinder.

And the children didn't stop running, even when the rain came down in floods. Hailstones bounced off their heads like missiles. The heaven's opened and poured down in rivulets from the leaves, drenching them to the skin. Stumbling and sliding on the muddy ground, they finally reached a familiar part of the woods. Three hours had passed by since the start of their journey.

'Keep going downwards,' instructed Peter. 'It's the only way to safety. If we can get to the "Blacksmith's Arms," and undercover, we'll be all right,' he added, panting for breath.

'I've got a stitch,' Vee said, doubling up in pain. 'Can't go on. Go without me. Take Charlie,' she gasped.

'Get your breath, then we'll all make a dash for it,' Eve said. Their legs were scratched and bleeding from the brambles. 'Don't forget. We're all for one and one for all!' The four musketeers slapped their hands onto each other's and feebly smiled. Vee looked at her companions' bloodied legs and realized she now had a one-in-four chance of being eaten alive by the dragon. These were much better odds. Another flash of lightning homed in above them on top of the ridge, causing them to crouch down. Then the thunder rumbled again.

'One. Two. Three. Four,' Peter counted. 'It's moving away. Come on. Let's go,' he urged, as sheet lightening filled the sky.

Exhausted and terrified, they finally reached the open tundra. Crossing the waterlogged highway, they clacked over the wooden bridge, across the railway track, past the factory furnaces, along the sodden cricket pitch and under the shelter of the porch of "The Blacksmith's Arms." Breathlessly their bodies heaved and puffed from the efforts of their escape, while Charlie completed a tactical manoeuvre and made a perfect landing, in spite of the storm.

'I'll get him next time!' he said firmly.

They shivered as the downpour pounded up from the pavement and flooded the drains. A deluge of surface water spurted out in fountains from the manhole covers in the middle of the road.

Slowly and quietly, the sky changed from black to a dull sulphureous yellow. Appearing through the oppressive atmosphere, a shaft of light shone into the woods above them. It's rays spread out like angel's wings and lifted the clouds to a different level. Then, as if by magic, a rainbow appeared.

'Look an angel has shushed the dragon back to sleep,' Charlie said in wonder, peering high above the factory roofs.

'I think you're right Charlie, 'Eve smiled. 'We've had a lucky escape. Just think we could have been burned to a crisp. Do you think anyone will believe us?'

"We'd best keep it quiet, else we shall all be in deep trouble. It'll be our special secret. O.K?' Peter replied.

As the rain eased off they left the cover of the porch and made their way back to the village, chattering with excitement. Everything steamed, including the children, as the prism of light vanished. The pavements gleamed after the cleansing rainfall, freed for a while from the factories indecorous actions.

'That had to be the best adventure ever,' Vee said, smiling broadly.

'Sure was. But how are we going to explain our missing cardies and hats? I'm never going back there again,' Eve said.

'I know,' said Charlie, cheekily. 'We'll say that you left them hanging on the garden fence, and Old Jude took them by mistake.' He knew their parents wouldn't believe that the dragon had blasted the forgotten items into cinders.

Say Hello Wave Goodbye

29th December.

She became more determined than ever, now that she'd made up her mind to rent the flat. One of her father's choice adages came into her head: "When one door closes another one opens." She decided to dress up and put in her contact lens for the second time in six months. Salt water doesn't go well with gas-permeable lens. A long suede skirt taken out from the back of the wardrobe. She had trouble fastening the zip and decided most definitely to take up aerobics in the New Year. The coffee coloured polo neck and the amber ear-rings Peter had bought her for her Sixteenth birthday, completed the outfit.

She zipped up high heeled boots, a little tight but worth the effort, then brushed her hair until it shone, sweeping it up into a French pleat. Eve looked in the mirror and was almost pleased with what she saw. Putting on her best brown cashmere coat and cream silk scarf, she outlined her full mouth with a soft peach lipstick. She then took up the Facial Steamer that Angela had bought her for Christmas. "Boots" would give her a refund. The Frizz-Relaxer, her birthday present, she put in the bin, thinking: Bitch! Now she was ready to the face the Estate Agents.

She inquired if the flat was still available. To her relief it was and paying the deposit, agreed to move in on 2nd January. The ex-council flat was nothing special: one bed. one bth. sitng room/ kitchntte, just a place to chill. For the first time in her life she would have, at least, a place of her own. As she left the agents she checked out a few brochure, noticing a cottage for sale. It was terraced, stone built and modernized throughout, with a small back garden and only

£15,000. Eve took the brochure recognizing the building. She had passed the row of cottages every day on her way to work.

Before she caught the bus back home she went into the Co-op and bought a radio/cassette, then had her lunch and a frothy Cappuccino in the Health Food Cafe, thinking to start her healthy eating habit early. The boots were killing her feet, so she slipped them off. A big mistake. The shop had already got Sale items in the windows. Christmas carols still sounded out through the speaker system on the clock tower. "Ding dong merrily on high..."

Browsing through the market stalls, with her boots only half zipped, she was stopped by a handsome young man dressed in a black suit and shiny shoes. He reminded her of Donny Osmond so she was surprised when he spoke in an American accent. As a Mormon preacher, he chatted to her for ages about his religion. She enjoyed a good discussion and felt particularly light-hearted when she returned back to 'Bleak House.'

Checking her reflection in the bathroom mirror she discovered with horror, a brown moustache of chocolate froth resting on her top lip. She thought of how cool the young man had acted. Never once had he focused on her mouth. Speaking in his soft accent with well-worn phrases, not even shown any sign of ridicule, or awareness of her moustache. Simply an intense young man bent on converting the ignorant. The bus driver had sneered, but that was nothing new.

Embarrassment became familiar to her. She thought of the time when Shirl showed her a photograph of her daughter as the Flower Fair. Little Julie stood behind the counter selling freesias. In front and taking up most of the frame was the back of a very large man, with a severely bad haircut. Eve unthinkingly said: 'What a pretty girl. Shame about the large headed man getting in the way.' Then she noticed Brenda's face, at the desk opposite, giving her the Oh! My! God! expression. Too late Eve realized that this enormous man was Shirl's dad.

Many times she'd been more embarrassed. Like the time a few years ago, when she wore one of her "Dynasty" style suits with

100

padded shoulders and tight skirt. She'd quickly jumped off the bus outside the Station, hoping not to miss the train. She'd walked around the office all day with a huge rip up the back of her skirt, exposing suspenders and stocking tops. Nobody said a word, until she had to take some forms to John Merton for signing. A lecher of the first order. As she left his office a strange gurgling sound came from his throat. Followed by a strangled groan. 'Your...skirt...it's... Oh! My! ...kind of split,' he said, breathing heavily.

Most recent and worst of all was her day-off trip to the big city. Thought she'd try the new shopping mall. She did some shopping and bought a ticket for the cinema. After leaving Mac.Donald's she took the escalator. It was then it happened. The tie cord in her velour pants, snapped. They were pink she remembered, with a matching short hooded top. Didn't notice, until she reached the top and tripped over, with the pants round her ankles. She stilled burned thinking about it. Wearing a thong with arse hanging in the breeze, in full view of the whole basement of the Meadowhall Centre, had to take the biscuit. She'd not returned since.

She took out the two creme caramels from the M & S carrier bag and felt guilty as hell for at least ten seconds. Then she kicked off the boots, sat in the recliner and spooned out the dark toffee from the bottom of the pot, deliberately ignoring the calorie count on the side. Working out that her 20% of the equity, would pay the deposit and get her some new furniture as well. She could just afford the monthly mortgage payments, making a note to view the cottage as soon as she had settled in the flat.

She'd been persuaded by the husband to make a verbal agreement, as the deeds were in his name. A 20% - 80% split of the proceeds. He would get £8,000, although she had supported him for four years, while he did his Teacher Training Diploma. He would give her £2,000.

The Funeral Emporium had come to an abrupt end when Old Gran blew herself up with the bunsen-burner one night, mixing one of her volatile concoction. The police put it down to the ignition of embalming fluid. Ironically her last words to Mitch before she locked herself in the cellar had been: 'I want cremating not burying. I don't want the worms eating me!' Most folks thought the worms had better taste. So her remains were re-ignited and cleansed in the fiery furnace - and Mitch inherited the business; which he quickly sold along with the house and furniture. With the proceeds of the sale they bought this house, taking the recliner as a solitary memento.

Eve sang softly as she made pasta sauce for herself and Anton. 'Volare.O O...Cantale O O O O,' stopping suddenly when the phone rang.

'Pronto!' said a high pitched giggling voice. 'Is that "Blind Pugh"?' One of her older sister's digs about Eve's short-sightedness. Angela sounded over cheerful. "Pronto" means 'Hello' in Italian you know... It's lovely here in Florence. Isn't it Meg?'

'How's Richard?' Eve managed to ask, her happy mood fading.

'He's landed on his feet here. Hasn't he Meg? Well, Maria's parents are loaded and we're staying in their house up in the mountains. They've gone for a walk with the dogs, so I'm cooking lunch. I've got a huge leg of lamb in the oven and have just beat up my Yorkshire Pudding mixture so I can't stop for long. Anyway Geoff and Keith are outside chopping logs for the fire oven and Richard is upstairs in his bedroom with Maria, listening to music... RICHARD CAN YOU TURN THAT RACKET DOWN! I CAN'T HEAR MYSELF THINK!...DO YOU WANT TO TALK TO YOUR AUNTIE EVIE?' Richard ignored his mother with his silence. 'Just like his father,' she moaned. 'Where was I? ...Oh! Yes! Sophia and Carlo think I'm lovely. Don't they Meg? You should see what they've bought us, must have cost a bomb.'

And so Angela prattled on about nothing for another hour, getting as many digs in as possible. 'You've never been to Italy have you Evie! We're going to the "Offices" after lunch to see some real paintings. Not those modern daubs that they do now!' Another dig. Angela knew Eve and Peter had decided to work in Italy, taking a year out before they went to university. They had planned to travel after passing their 'A' levels. Eve was to study Art and Peter Architecture.

Eve thought: It's "The Uffizi," you bitch, but didn't correct her sister.

The family had always ignored Angela's tantrums and sarcasm, because if they responded she would never let them hear the end of it. Twisting the story so that she became the victim. Meg and Eve had learned to keep their mouths closed; regardless. There could only be one winner in Angela's world - and ultimately, she was harmless.

Angela ran out of steam, but then got her second wind. 'You'll never guess who we bumped into yesterday? Go on try?' Eve remained silent.

'PEETRILL!' she declared, empowered by her knowledge. Eve's heart quickened.

'There he was sat outside a cafe, drinking coffee with this beautiful young Italian girl... Wasn't he Meg? She was about sixteen with long black hair, really slim and ever so brown. You know, like me when I've been to Sicily!'

Eve knew only to well about Angela's white bits as she showed them to anyone who would look, at the same time putting her brown arm against her sister's white one and calling her "Bucket Chops." Eve got this nickname, among many from Angela, when she was twelve. She asked her sister what she meant and she'd explained, laughing: 'BUCKET CHOPS! ...PALEFACE!'

Angela had always treated her younger sister with indifference, until Eve reached the age of twelve. Ballet and gymnastics had streamlined her body, giving her a gracefulness and unimposing charm. She had grown two inches taller than Angela so she no longer was called "Titch". They'd all got dressed up for Angela's Engagement party and Eve had a powder blue flared dress, some blue china 'dangler' ear-rings and her first pair of high heels. Meg had styled her hair into a chignon of curls. So when Eve walked into the sitting room to show her parents they both looked at each other and smiled.

Angela was sitting on Keith's knee, when he made an innocent remark for which she never forgave him. 'My what a looker Evie has turned into!' From that day forth Angela punished Eve relentlessly - incapable of marring the image in her mind of Keith's total adoration!

'It turns out that this girl is Peter's daughter and he's divorced.

If it wasn't for my Keithy I'd have been in there. He always fancied me. Didn't he Meg? Anyway I've got to put my puddings in the oven. Our Richard says no one can make Yorkshire Puddings like me!... Ciao!.. Here talk to our Evie...' she said, handing the phone to Meg.

'Hello love. You all right? Take no notice of her she's been at the Chiante,' said Meg kindly. 'Have you decided what you're going to do yet?' she whispered.

'Yes I have Meg. If you don't mind I'm going to take the flat, until I can buy something.'

'That's all right love. As long as you know what you're doing. There's always a room for you at our house.'

'Meg?'

'Yes?'

'Did Peter say anything about me?'

'Well he tried to ask how you were but our Angela kept interrupting.'

'Did you tell him that I was getting divorced?'

'I tried to whisper it to him, but she was ear-wigging all the time. And I know you didn't want her to find out until things were settled. I best be off now love, because Sophia and Carlo are back. I'll see you on the 2nd.'

'Love you Sis,' Eve said.

'Me too - and Geoff... Bye.' What Meg didn't tell her was that they'd all caught ring-worm from the four enormous German shepherd dogs, that insisted on sleeping on their beds.

Sorting through the few tapes the husband left behind, she noted he'd been very selective. Phil Collins, Dire Straits, Bob Dylan, Bruce Springfield, Kate Bush, Judy Collins, all missing. Behind he'd left: Clannad, Whales Songs, Buddhists Chants, Rod Stewart, and Bob Dylan's one and only religious crap album: "Saved." She tuned in the radio instead and Cliff was giving it full throttle with "It's so funny How we don't talk anymore."

'Try again.' The maestro's instantly recognizable sound. 'Bob Dylan, that's more like it.'

"Tell me How does it feel To be on your own Like a complete unknown..."

'Come on Bobby give me a break!'

Radio 4. 'That's better'. Mozart subliminal chords. "Clarinet Concerto in A Major."

Eve went to check on the sauce and give it stir when there was a knock on the back door. She looked through the kitchen window at the shiny red Sierra on the drive, wondering who it belong to. A familiar looming outline stood close to the opaque glass. It was Mitch all dressed up in suit and tie and smiling his lop-sided smile. Quickly she hid the radio in the cupboard. She didn't trust him. She guessed the car belonged to his girlfriend. He'd driven around in 'The Yellow Ferret' Ford Anglia for years, tying up the exhaust with string and stuffing the hole in the passenger seat with an old blanket.

'What do you want?' she asked, peering from behind the door and feeling nervous.

'I need to talk to you. Can I come in?'

Eve beckoned him in and put the kettle on. 'Take a seat!' she said, nodding at the deck-chair and recliner.

'I'd rather stand if you don't mind,' he said sheepishly, walking into the lounge.

'The back garden looks nice,' he added, trying to make conversation.

'Is it still three sugars?' she asked.

He nodded. As she stirred the coffee, she noticed Anton creeping in front of the car with a crowbar. When he raised it up and starting smashing the headlights she turned the kettle back on to cover the noise. 'What are you doing?' she mouthed through the window. Anton chuckled and put his finger to his mouth to shush her quiet, then disappeared.

Eve took the coffee into the lounge and put it on the window sill. 'Biscuit?' she asked in a forced civilized voice.

'Yes please!'

She returned to the kitchen and put some biscuits on a plate and turned the sauce down to simmer. Anton was now sweeping up the glass with a brush and pan, then vanished again. Thought she heard him mutter something like, 'Nazi Bastard!' under his breath.

'Eve! I've been thinking. I really miss you and I want us to give it another go-'

'What!?'

'Just hear me out.' He placed his hand on her shoulder in that old oppressive way and said. 'When I get my money...Err... I mean our money, I'm going to save it and look for a new house. Then I'll come and find you. You want that don't you?'

Eve was just about to tell him where to stick the 'new house,' when she saw Anton shoveling something onto a spade in his back garden, then walking back towards the car. 'Wait a minute I need some more milk in my coffee...Help yourself to biscuits.'

Mitch smiled. Enjoying the aroma of simple food. Thinking everything was going to plan. While outside Anton slid the shovel through the open window of the car and dropped something onto the seat. She gestured for him to back off, but he just chuckled and disappeared round the other side. He took the shovel and scraped it along the passenger door for good measure, then walked away singing.

Mitch realized what he'd lost. His comfortable Eve. She never nagged. Never made him do chores. Never asked for anything. Didn't make him wear a thong. She'd waited patiently for him to be a real man. Well now he would be, he thought. It wasn't too late to start again. Have children. And she did look nice, with her hair like that. Her long hair-free legs, smooth and shiny. Small beautifully shaped feet. He not noticed them before. Her golden skin, shining with light. She seemed really serene. He though he'd heard her singing. The sound of happy music. Then he felt embarrassed. How could there be any music. He'd taken the stereo. She'd not even complained. The chase stirred him into life.

All he had now was a woman who never let him alone. No time to think. No time to read, dream - or sleep. Julie the small dark-haired bony woman, with a six pack. Rabbit! Rabbit! Talked quickly and nervously. She'd seduced him. Got him when he was vulnerable. Now he did everything possible to avoid her. Stayed up late until she fell asleep. Left for school early to elude the arguments. She was sex mad. He couldn't do anything right. Not even when they made love. She told him how to do it. To think of his 13 times table. It would prolong ejaculation. She screamed the house down, when she climaxed. It scared him. He couldn't cope. Worse during the holiday breaks. Around him all the time. And here was his cuddly Eve still waiting for him to be a real man, he thought.

When Eve returned, Mitch smiled at her. 'What I'm asking is - will you still be my wife, before the "Absolute" comes through?' He came nearer to Eve and put his sinewy hands on her shoulders again. 'You look almost pretty in this light,' he said.

Even this back handed compliment didn't hurt. His throw away sarcasm used to cut her deeply. It just wasn't important what he thought, or did, anymore. She had an overwhelming desire to hit him.

She surveyed the vast expanse of his stomach. Then looking up she could see thick black hairs in his nose, suddenly realizing how huge it was from that perspective and that he wasn't totally albino after all. It was at that premonitory moment Eve fell totally out of love with Mitch, when the pendulum swung to its polar opposite. Only when another woman fancied the Soon-to-be-ex did he become attractive to her. Once more the many facets of human nature showed themselves in paradoxical forms. In her former desperation, the Greek god she thought lost forever, was now in the cold light of day, no more than the manipulative, mean, ex- embalmer she'd always known. A sad prat who had been dominated by the Wicked Witch of the West and was now worn out by Miss Whiplash.

'What colour are my eyes Mitch?' she asked looking at his ample waist.

'Err. Um. Bluish?' he grinned.

'They're green...You arsehole. Now get out of 'your' house and go back to Miss Whiplash. She'll have your dinner on the table, so you'd better not be late!' She wanted to say more. All the things he'd done to hurt her, bottled up inside. The unfairness of it all. Let out the anger. But right at that moment: "Least said soon is mended," sprung into her head. Bugger!

Mitch was stunned to the core. She didn't use to swear. Never got angry. Must have changed. Just like Julie Bossy-Drawers, waiting for his return. Probably wearing a leather cat-suit and sharpening her claws. Jesus. Go to Mac. Donald's instead. Spin out the time. A few games of snooker. Stay out extra late. Creep in quietly. Put some 'Quiet Life' tablets in her coffee. She'd be asleep by the time he got home, he hoped. He stumbled out of the house, flopping down in a huff into the cat-poo, then reversed out of the drive and sped away to the strains of: '... "We don't need no thought control/No dark sarcasm in the classroom/teacher Leave those kids alone."

He had to return to his new abode to change. Feigned illness. Invented a headache. Oiled the door-hinges when she wasn't looking. Escaped quickly. Pushed by her as she leaned provocatively against the door, blocking his way. Hell's Bells! Didn't she ever think of anything else but sex? His willy definitely needed a rest. That night he phoned from the Snooker Hall, very drunk. Told Eve she could whistle for her money. He was going to blow the lot! "Enough is as good as a feast," drifted into her head. One of her father's sayings, again. Why Dad? Why is enough good enough? Aren't we to expect anything more? Then she smiled, acknowledging the wisdom. She would manage. For certain she didn't need the Soon-to-be-ex's money. He could stuff it where the sun didn't shine, but she doubted there would be room. The tight-arsed bastard.

'Never minding luff. What you never be having what you never be missing!' Anton comforted her. 'I would loving to be seeing his face though, when he getting out of car with cat shit on pants.'

Music To Watch Girls By

When Eve started senior school she still called for Vee every morning. This time they had a long bus ride in front of them. Peter walked from the old village to join them at the bus shelter. They were all very nervous, wearing their brand new uniforms. Struggling with the starched shirts and ties. The girls in maroon and powder blue, while the boys wore black with white shirts. For the first time they were to be segregated. The concept of single sex schools was simple. Put boys in cages and girls in ivory towers. Let them to burn off excess energy with frantic games and sports twice a day. Played in separate fields during staggered hours. Rampant hormones denied. Objective achieved.

After a long journey, followed by a trek uphill, the boys went slowly through the first pillared drive and the girls walked some fifty yards to their side of the school. Peter waved and the other boys laughed at him. He wasn't ready to let go. He needed to hear the girlish laughter of his friends, became confused by this sudden change. Children trapped in the middle-earth battle between Victorian morals and post-War modernism.

Meg and Angela left school at the age of fifteen. None of the Blackridge children passed the 11+ exams. Unable to understand most of the questions, it spoiled their chances of anything better. Shop workers or factory girls, were their choices. Eve's generation had more opportunities. A chance to go on to college to take 'O' levels. These changes made it possible for the village children to better themselves. Or, at least, they had the opportunity to give it a try.

The red brick Victorian building was divided into two halves. The top section designed for the boys, and the lower sealed off, for the girls. The sound of feet clattering above their heads the only reminder of 'Kiss-catch' in the school yard. The two sexes met up as they walked back and forth to school. Even then they weren't supposed to speak to each other. Emulate ladies and gentlemen. Act demure. Avoid physical contact. Ignore any attempts at vocal interaction.

Annexes built on the boys side of the playing fields, soon changed everything. The small workrooms designed for Arts ands Crafts. Two young female Beatnik art teachers arrived, wearing black nail polish and very long earrings. Miss Oxborough and Miss Daniels were Goths extraordinary.

Eve was in her element in the updated creative section. She painted freestyle with gusto. Much to the delight of the girls, they now walked across the boys playground at the rear of the school, for the first time. Miss Moseley soon wiped the smiles off their faces. Instructed to 'turn heads left' so they wouldn't see any males. They thought it extremely weird. Walking in a straight line to the annexes with heads turned towards the playing fields, caused a few trippings up. And a great deal of giggling and peeping followed. Every single lesson and break expertly coordinated so the sexes kept apart.

When they got inside the building it was a different matter. Miss Moseley faded into the distance on her return to sanctuary. She'd got bow legs from rickets and an arse like a grazing buffalo. The sudden excitement reminded Eve of Wagon Train. Their dash for freedom to find pastures new in the promised land. Each girl staking their claim to her own space. Mixing paints, making a mess. Left the blobs to dry. The next colourful reminders for other girls to add their daubs. The Teachers mavericks and the girls palamino. All of the girls rushed into class to put on their painting aprons. They could be as noisy as they liked. Paint whatever they wanted. Finger daubs, abstracts, sunsets, cutting out, gluing. Twinkle, sparkle and tinsel. They even coloured in the windows. All the while they tried to get a glimpse of the boys in their shorts, on the playing fields. The teachers back at the ranch never found out about the goings on in the annexes.

Vee was in a different grade to Eve. It was like separating Siamese twins. At playtime they caught up on the day's events. All the first years got a clip from the older girls. 'First Year Clip!' they shouted, asserting their power. They endured slaps round the head, until the bell clanged out. Vee and Eve couldn't understand why there wasn't a queue for the six toilets in the yard, shared by hundreds of girls. Revolting summed them up. No toilet paper. Forgotten outreaches. They all learned bladder control, until they returned home. The Blackridge girls made new friends from other catchment areas, but still traveled and played together.

The bus service to the village was infrequent: one every 45 minutes. The Blackridge children were always late for school. The Late Monitor waited at the top of each drive, grimacing when they said: 'Blackridge.' Others learned to say the same to avoid getting a late mark. Also the village children got a bad name on the bus service, because they stampeded to get onboard. They all pushed and shoved into each other in one mass. What the conductress didn't realize was that the kids panicked. If the bus was full, especially on Winter evenings, they'd have to wait another 45 minutes in the cold.

All the teachers were females. The majority of them were Misses, very ancient and very peculiar. They didn't give out physical punishment. Instead the girls got Bad Marks on their reports and detentions. Eve and Vee only got one bad mark the whole time they attended. It was the first Christmas when Miss Stafford struck up a jaunty tune on the piano. "The Holly and The Ivy." Some of the older girls started singing different words: 'Our teacher is a funny 'un With a head like a Spanish onion A face like a squash tomato And legs like two props...'

Vee and Eve always tried to sit near each other in assembly. They hadn't heard this alternative version before and laughed out loud. Pamela Conway told the teacher they were the culprits. Both girls were gutted when they got their first Bad Mark. Vee and Eve got their revenge. They stitched the sleeves of her coat together and put itching powder in her P.T. kit. The days were tedious as the old ladies droned on. Every lesson laced with righteousness. Music Lessons were more fun. If the girls asked to listen to Italian Opera on the old wind-up gramophone, they knew they didn't have to do any work. Miss Stafford, as mad as a hatter, drove an old Ford Popular. She sat in her classroom transfixed by Caruso and Gigli, tears pouring from her red roumy eyes. Lost in her dreams. Her hatchet face belied her unfulfilled soul. She returned to the world only when the bell rang out. During the hour long lesson the girls made sure the gramophone never wound down.

Miss Stafford lived with Miss Sidebottom. The latter was very deaf and wore a huge hearing aid, with a giant battery pack hanging from her neck. She taught Science. The girls played the same jokes on Miss Sidebottom and she always fell for them. Pranks handed down in the oral tradition. The poor woman suffered for years. They would mouth their words to her, knowing she would turn up her hearing aid. When the device was on full volume, they'd shout out the answers. Often they complained of a gas smell from the bunsen-burners. The Science Lab cleared out, until the 'leak' was traced. It worked every time.

The Needlework teacher Miss Cartwright defied gravity. She was five feet wide and four feet tall, slightly balding with a wide centre parting and bad dandruff. Her favourite pupils were the big girls. Eve struggled to use a treddle sewing machine. She couldn't get the rhythm. Her newly made cookery apron and cap askew. Miss Cartwright made the pretty girls pick up the pins with magnets, at end of the lesson. Boasted that she'd taught Sabrina, a girl on the Arthur Askey show on television with enormous bosoms. Vee said: 'I bet she had to pick up the pins.'

Mrs. Earnshaw, the Scripture teacher: a tyrant by profession. Made the girls learn twenty verses from The Bible every week. Determined to ruin their weekends. On Monday's she'd paced up and down the aisles, terrifying them. Face unsmiling. Teeth gritted. Cheeks sucked in. Then randomly selected a girl to recite the verses, by tapping her on the shoulder. If she made a mistake, she got twenty more to learn. Vee and Eve longed for Mr. Marsh. They'd had no one to sigh over, until they saw a Third Year boy called 'Cab' Baum. Every leather satchel became emblazoned with his name. His reputation was so astounding that even those who had never set eyes on him, still wrote his name in bold letters. Relying on other girls' description of his good looks. Lelia Hastings said he had the longest winkle-pickers and the shortest 'bum-freezer' jacket, when she saw him at the Dance Hall in town. He asked her to bop. She said that he was an amazing mover: 'Just like Elvis.' When she showed everyone her love-bite the girls were extremely envious. They practiced on each other. Showing their bruise marks at playtime and concealing them during lessons. Lelia did have breasts before everyone else though. And she did ask Cab to bite her.

On their first day the Head Girl came into their class, as Mrs. Mooney's presence was requested by the mad Welsh Headmistress. The Head Girl built like a tank and a brilliant swimmer. She also had a man's booming voice. 'Whom of you have siblings at this school?' Nobody answered. They didn't know the meaning of the word. 'Come along... Surely some of you have sisters who attended this institution?'

Eve shot her hand up. 'Yes Miss... My sister: Angela Watts. She left last Christmas.'

'I hope you are better behaved than your sister,' the big girl replied disapprovingly. She didn't say anything good about anyone else's sisters either. From that moment the whole class took an instant dislike to 'Hairy Hazel.' Especially when she wrote on the blackboard the word: Antidisestablishmentantarianism. Then told them to make as many words as they could from it. She said it was the longest word in the English language. No matter how hard they tried they never managed to find the word in their dictionaries.

The quiet girl sitting next to Eve, called Annmarie said: 'She's a big-headed, fat-arsed pillock.'
Eve warmed to her immediately.

So when 'Hairy Hazel' in her elasticized swimming costume won all the County trophies for speed swimming at the Annual Gala, she only got a half hearted cheer. The final race brought the house down, during the back butterfly, as Hazel Brentford's enormous breast escaped from the ever-shrinking costume. A daring stroke only she would attempt. Her breast made a bid for freedom. Either side of the contracted strip, they thrust out above the surface of the water, bobbing around like two large footballs. Nevertheless she continued and won the race, to thunderous applause. The Mayor overcome with excitement, nearly fell off his seat.

Miss Blodwyn Jones the Headmistress, was another matter. The whole school laughed at her eccentricities, behind her back. She had grey plaits wrapped in swirls, glued either side of her head, like large

113

Catherine wheels. She greeted the girls in assembly with Pranown Dar and Borra Dar, before giving her sermons. She was an enormous mountain of a woman, with a tent for a dress, trimmed with long jet beads. Her moustache rivaled David Niven's. She waved her arms about in her religious fervor, stomach undulating. Saying every single day: 'And...the ungodly shall perish in the Fires of Damnation.' It sounded poetic with her powerful Welsh lilt. Everyone shook with fear, except for the Godley sisters, who looked quite embarrassed.

When Eve joined The Civic Offices, she later found out that the screw-loose Headmistress, spent most of her time sitting in her cosy office, in front of a glowing fire. The rest of the school shivered.

The Education Officer visited the Headmistress on many an occasion. He always drew the short straw. She would shout: 'Who goes there?' If the person answered was someone she didn't want to see, she remained silent. None of the staff, or children, dare enter without being asked. For some reason she liked softly spoken Mr. Reynolds, The Education Officer. 'Enter!'

He saw her Queen Anne legs up on the desk, revealing an expanse of pink silk bloomers. She reclined Rubenesque, eating Jaffa oranges. She spat the pips into the fire periodically, then commenced speaking in between about the bad manners of the girls. The floor littered with peel. It was owing to this particular conversation the Education Officer arranged elocution lessons for the A Forms. The water fountain was directly outside her window and she despised the way the girls spoke in their Yorkshire dialect.

'Despicable is it. Look you,' she said.

For weeks the girls recited: Louis laid a long ladder lengthwise on the lawn and Round the rugged rock the ragged rascal ran. Gloria Sweeney got a certificate for Good Articulation. Poor Nina Sanders rolled her R's and developed a nervous twitch in Miss Laycock's Elocution classes. When the final bell rang out the girls walked sedately in twos, out of the building. As soon as the school was out of sight, berets and ties were taken off, and coats were unbuttoned. The girls tried to walk like Lelia, swaying their hips, and the boys curled their lips like Elvis/Cab. The only good things about the long walk back to the bus stop at the bottom of the hill, were the sweet shop and the bakers. After school each afternoon, the kids would buy penny loaves, still warm and poke out the soft bread from the middles. After these were eaten they'd filled the crispy shells with a shared bag of crisps.

It was nearing Christmas and the selection of angels for the Christmas play was imminent. All the girls wanted to be Mother Mary or angels. Eve knew she and Vee didn't stand a chance. The teachers only picked girls with blonde hair. No one wanted to be Joseph. Pat Kirbridge the tallest girl in the class, walked around with bent knees and a stoop to avoid selection. She got the role of one of the Three Kings. Instead Eve and Vee were allowed to trim up the Christmas tree and make paper chains for the Hall.

It was the same procedure during dancing lessons. Eve, taller than Annmarie, never learned to dance backwards. They were told off for bobbing up and down, by Miss Wilton. 'Glide girls. Glide! And bend the knees.' Julie Lockwood had ballet lessons and her legs were muscular and lithesome. She could hold three-penny bits between her thighs, calves and ankles, all at the same time. The other girls tried to do the same and failed. Some time later, when the girls studied 'Romeo and Juliet' they noted a heavily blacked out phrase. If they held the book up to the light they could see the words. It read: 'quivering thigh.' After that they didn't care about Julie's taut legs. Nevertheless, poker backed she danced to perfection. 'Everyone! Watch Julie and Sarah. They glide beautifully.' Julie didn't learn to dance backwards either - and she played Joseph. Later they also discovered a deleted 'full-bellied' in their Shakespeare texts. The big girls also had cause to feel happy.

Eve couldn't recollect any bitchiness from her Halcyon days at the Waterwell School for Girls. They all looked alike and dressed the same. Hair worn in either: bunches, plaits or a basin cut. Gym slips, shirts and ties and lace up shoes. Unless, that is, they had hair like Eve. Even the beret didn't flatten it into submission. Sprang back to life as soon as the pancake hat came off. On good days her mother made finger curls and tied a section back with a ribbon. It stayed this way in temperate weather, but any sign of a mist and the hair went wild again. Rose patiently raked the locks every morning with water, in preparation for the ringlets. Then one day a boy walking behind Eve called out: 'Look at chuffing Shirley Temple!' She wore her hair in a tight pony tail after that.

Eve clearly remembered the last day before the Christmas holidays. The rich fruit cakes they'd made in Cookery Class were ready for icing. She had a snowman and a robin, and a red ribbon for decoration. The cookery teacher, Miss Howlett, quite often gave them wrong instructions. She was the sort of woman that never finished her sentences. Her thoughts seemed to trail off somewhere else. She resembled Boris Kharloff sans make-up. Her claw hands textured like dead leaves, fascinated. When she rubbed them together, covered in flour, the sound was like the ghost of Cathy scratching the window in "Wuthering Heights." This always made the girls wince.

Naturally everyone's icing came out too runny. She forgotten to tell them to beat the egg whites until stiffened. This supposedly made the icing sugar fluffy like peaks of snow. Too much sugar and water reversed the effect. It was flat and sticky.

Eve had forgotten the cake tin, to carry it home. Miss Howlett gave her a brown paper bag to cover it. Wished her 'Happy Easter' and hoped it didn't rain. She, Vee and Peter decided to walk home, rather than risk dropping the cake in the mad rush to get onto the bus. The Christmas Holidays began and they shouted out in relief and excitement. By the time she got home after an hour's walk, the cake had squashed flat and most of the icing had congealed inside the brown paper. The robin and the red ribbon turned the wet icing into a pale shade of pink. The snowman must have fallen out at some point, when she nearly fell over. It must have been when she'd tripped near the Sewerage Works on Meadowland as the bus whizzed past them. Children inside wiped the steamed up windows to get a better view. Ted banged on the window and gave them a royal wave. The cake weighed a ton. Fortunately, at that moment, Peter caught her by the arm, otherwise the cake would definitely have perished. By this time all three of them laughed heartily at the thought of the cake flying over the iron railings and landing in the sewage. Vee caused more hilarity, when she said: 'The Careers Officer asked our Ted what he wanted to be…He replied that he wanted to be a Sewerage Diver! He got into big trouble.'

'Never mind Evie love. We'll soon fix it,' her mother said smiling, when she saw the ruined offering. Eve's face showed her disappointment. 'My, you're freezing. Come on sit yourself by the fire and I'll make you a hot drink,' Rose said, rubbing her daughter's hands. 'Then we'll sort out the little problem...Don't you worry. It'll be the best Christmas cake ever.'

After Eve had warmed herself through, her mother cleared the table and studied the disastrous icing. She scraped of the soggy mess and threw it in the bin. Whipped three egg whites up into stiff peaks. Then folded some fresh icing sugar into the mixture. Fortunately the almond paste held the cake together. Her mother skillfully applied the icing with a spatula, pulling it away quickly to form snow drifts. The lonesome faded robin was set on high and a skirt made out of green Christmas tinsel fitted round the circumference. A dab of cochineal added to a thicker mixture, then 'Merry Christmas' iced in the centre. A few delicately iced Christmas roses gave it a little more colour, with tiny edible silver balls pressed into the snowy layers. The Restoration work completed before tea time. Eve conceded her mother knew more about baking than Miss Howlett. The icing set rock hard on the pantry slab and the whole family complimented her on the fruity taste of the cake. Miss Howlett had overestimated the glacier cherries, but no one complained.

Walls Come Tumbling Down

The fifth paperweight, or course, Millifiori she thought, remembering what Mrs. Pinkerton had told her on her Thirteenth birthday. Her mother, Angela and she had firstly gone to the Attercliffe Christmas market. The whole stretch of road had been closed for hundreds of stalls, decked out in Christmas lights. The murky street transformed into something extraordinarily beautiful. Angela bought a pair of black silk stockings with a seam all the way up the back. Rose wanted some indigestion tablets from the chemist, so they all went inside.

Eve studied the large fat bellied glass jars on the top shelf, each containing different coloured liquid. She wondered what they were used for, then decided they were simply for decorative purposes.

'HAVE YOU GOT ANY BLACK- HEAD SQUEEZERS?' Angela asked in a very loud voice, as her mother paid for the tablets.

'Surely it's not for you?' the chemist queried, looking at Angela's rosy cheeks.

'No!' she laughed. 'It's for her over there!' She nodded towards Eve. She wanted the floor to open up and swallow her. Angela paid for the implement and gave it to her embarrassed sister saying. 'Here you are "Turnip Head"!'

'Oh! Angela. For goodness sake!' her mother chided.

Eve ran out of the shop, saying to her mother, 'I'm going to Mrs. Pinkerton's stall. See you later.'

She ran all the way to the Fairground, with tears streaming down her face. Hating her sister for her cruel jibes. Feeling like a complete idiot for not giving back some of the taunts. Then she decided it wasn't worth it. Angela would never let it rest and things would be worse than before.

Mrs. Pinkerton was dressed in sky blue with matching Alice

band and large crescent moonstone earrings. Her hair seemed bigger and shone blue black under the lights, emphasizing the whiteness of her face.

'Hello flame-haired child!' Mrs. Pinkerton called. 'Why the tears?'

'It's nothing. I've got something in my eye,' she said, sniffing.

'Have you come to buy your Birthday present?' Eve nodded. Mrs. Pinkerton brought out the most beautiful paperweight to date. It looked like the inside of seaside rock, but had hundreds of different colours flashing through it.

'See here... Look! It has a thousand flowers inside. "Millifiori" in Italian,' she said, handing the glass dome over the Eve. 'One shilling darling for your future happiness.' Mrs. Pinkerton was being all mysterious again, so Eve forgot about her hurt pride for a moment. 'Take the dome and dream of Italia! Study it carefully... Paint a picture in your mind and see how it can happen. Be lucky my dove!'

Eve returned home and put the paperweight in the bottom drawer with the others, to keep it safe, but forgot about the gypsy's words. She still smarted from Angela's cruelty. Determined to eat more cakes after Angela had greeted her with "Sparrow legs" is back!'

Meg and her mother sat either side of the fire place, smiling at each other. The kitchen cosy and warm, bathed in firelight. In the middle of the hearth rug was a large cardboard box. 'What's inside?' she asked.

'Why don't you look and see?' her mother said.

She knew it was a special birthday present because of the expression on her mother's face. Lifting the deep lid she exposed layers and layers of tissue paper. This in itself was something she'd not seen before. How it rustled in the firelight. She put this to one side and the cat Nero, jumped in the middle and settled down for a sleep. Lying at the bottom of the box was a thing of beauty. Almost like a bride's dress. It had a satin underskirt with a layer of stiffened chiffon edge in white silk, over the top. A ribbon of silk fastened round the waist and the tiny cap sleeves were also edged in the same material.

'Come on then love. Try it on. It's been put by with Mrs. Brocklehurst for ages,' her mother urged, almost as excited as Eve.

'I've booked for you to have your picture taken at Cecil's Studios.'

'Do you like it Evie?' Meg asked.

'It's the most beautiful dress I've ever seen. Thanks Mum,' she said, hugging her mother. Knowing how she must have scrimped and saved to pay for it. She also decided to have her photograph taken sitting down, in case anyone saw her 'sparrow legs.'

Angela left the house to meet Keith. She had stitched herself inside black drainpipe trousers to make them tighter on the calves. Her shocking pink socks, lipstick, and large hoop-earrings, glowed in the dark. They matched her duffle coat. Tonight she would cut herself out of the trousers again. She left shouting: 'See ya!' muttering a few choice phrases under her breath. Exasperated by the attention her younger sister received, she slammed the door behind her.

Stan gathered up the tissue paper and cut it into small squares. It was threaded with string and hung on the back of the outside toilet door. They usually had the "Green Un," newspaper to contend with. The best Izal toilet roll was for upstairs.

Angela's marriage to Keith was imminent. The house buzzed from her laughter and excitement. Adam Faith was singing on the radio, "What do you want If you don't want money?" She and Keith bobbed around the kitchen in the jerky pump-handle style of the Fifties. The whole family clapped in time to the music as Dwayne Eddie followed Adam, singing: "Come on Everybody..," The couple moved well together. Entertaining the family and embarrassing their grand-children right into old age.

Eve, and Keith's sister Gladys, were the bridesmaids. Angela chose red thinking it would clash terribly with Eve's hair. In daylight the fabric had an amber tinge. Meg said it suited her perfectly.

The wedding was a riotous affair held in Highbank Church Hall. Keith's family came from the rougher end of Attercliffe in Sheffield. Both families agreed to hold the wedding just over the boundary. Neutral territory. He was the only boy amid seven sisters, who were all feisty, very small and exceptionally loud.

The first time Angela met her prospective father-in-law, Alf Riley, she was wearing a pair of tight ski-pants. He shook her hand and said: 'There's not much bleeding ball space in them luv,' looking at her crotch. That was a taste of things to come. Angela loved his

120

bad mannered insults. Alf didn't give a toss about whom he offended - and he could eat an apple without wearing dentures.

Alf Riley's, real name was Alfonso O'Riley. An Irish gypsy who had traveled with Muldoon's Fairground, since the day he was born. When the fair came to Sheffield, Alfonso fell in love with Beatrice, an auburn-haired girl from Attercliffe. She persuaded him to settle for a well paid job undercover in the Crucible Steel Works. A factory that produced the finest steel on the planet; although the Spanish disputed this claim on every occasion.

Every so often young Alfonso went walk-about. His quick mind, itching feet and adventurous spirit rejected containment. He traveled in his horse-drawn caravan, which he kept on a piece of spare land behind the smoking chimneys, during 'settled' times. On his journeys he did everything and anything to earn a crust. The ladies found his wild handsome looks irresistible. The way he swaggered about. How his black curls fell over his shoulders. His deep sensual eyes. Spinsters fainted. Daughters were locked up. Husbands acted jealous. Boyfriends became more attentive. All these things managed to turn their ordinary lives upside down. There are many of Alfonso good looking descendants scattered around The British Isles.

What Alfonso didn't know about horses you could write on the head of a pin. He had the gift. He could talk the talk. In the wilds of Derbyshire his services were indispensable to the horsy set. The Tamer of Horses, King of Gypsies, Seducer of Virgins, Slayer of Dragons, Tango Champion, Ambassador of the Underdog, Queller of Riots and Infinite Imbiber, were a few of his titles. Everyone was fascinated with the Alfonso.

As Alfonso gradually disappeared with age, Alf became the local ragman. He took up pigeon racing. Often times operating on the egg-bound birds, then stitching them up with twine. His accent a hybrid of many dialects, all seasoned with irreverence. Then his son, Keith took up the baton from the wild rover, until meeting Angela.

During the Wedding Ceremony Rose and Stan were uncomfortable with the raucous banter, punctuated with lots of 'bleeding' and 'bollocking' words. Rose wore her 'swivel(chisel)toe shoes and trifle(tricel) suit with an orghandi (organza) hat.' The shoes were too big but she'd said: 'They'll be all right just for walking about in.' Whereas Keith's family dressed casual and thought the new in-laws stuck up. Rose had already caused a stir in church, by singing: 'And the skies were filled with ruptures(raptures),' causing Stan to have a coughing fit. As Angela took her vows her shoulders were jigging up and down with restrained laughter.

As the reception got into full swing, Keith's sister Gladys, the chief bridesmaid, started an argument with her cousin, over from Ireland. When the barmaid came over and asked her to lower her voice, she smacked her right on the nose, calling her a: 'Bleeding nosy fat chuff!'

Then the barman, her husband, ran to the poor woman's defense. He was also attacked, for butting in. Mayhem, then pandemonium ensued. Eve's family cleared a space around the feuding in-laws, except for Auntie Dot, a red-head who loved a good set to. While Keith's Uncle Bob continued on the piano with his selection of tunes from "The Sound of Music," Catholic uncle Patrick rolled over the top of the keyboard clutching the throat of the C. of E. church warden, swearing furiously. Bob, undeterred, continued to tinkle the ivories around the them. It was during 'What are we going to do about Maria?' the three tier wedding cake collapsed. Felled by a fat fist on the icing sugar bride and groom, that penetrated all the way down through the almond paste into rich fruit mixture. Geoff intervened. 'Enough already!' he shouted standing in between two exhausted red-faced men.

Eventually full order was restored by retired 'Bobby' P.C. Stonehouse, who had also made and iced the cake, blowing his whistle and calling out: 'Half-time!'...The drinks are on me!' Then he slipped a ten shilling note to the barman, for damages.

Angela loved every minute and from that day on learned to curse, spit and swear in the Attercliffe/Irish genre. Keith reluctantly forsook the fairground and worked with Geoff and Stan in the factory. He grew a neat black beard at Angela's insistence and was ever after called, 'Jesus', by his work-mates. Geoff was in the 'Tool Shop' and did skilled work, but Keith took up grinding and knocked out badly, but quickly done crankshafts by the dozen, earning more money than the others. The best dressed man on the block. Stan, the girls' father, drove the overhead crane, since his accident and was quite happy up there alone with his thoughts.

For weeks after her birthday Eve tried to squeeze the 'black heads' round her nose, with the implement of torture, making it red and raw, until her mother eventually noticed. She told her they were merely freckles and threw it in the bin.

Let It Snow

The snow had fallen thick and fast that winter, fattening the sullied earth and turning the valley into virginal whiteness. None of the kids in the village had sledges so anything and everything sufficed for transport. Stretching from Mission Grange down to Abbots Lane was a steep slope, polished to perfection. A sheet of solid white ice smoothed the way. It didn't matter if the odd car couldn't get up there. Most people didn't mind walking.

The snow covered roofs of neat Council houses looked picture postcard. Set in twos with concrete post threaded with wire, to mark out the boundaries. Some three hundred souls resided there. A few shops set at the top of the estate including, the Co-op in the middle. A mobile butcher and "Vinegar Man" called once a week. At this moment nothing disturbed the peace, not even the milkman managed to get through the deep drifts. They were all held in the silent grip of winter.

Then with the din of sliding and slipping, the games started. Eve and Vee tried cardboard boxes at first, until they got soggy. One kid had a metal tea tray that went like the clappers. He held on and prayed, hoping to avoid the gas lamp at the bottom. Little Jimmy Reynolds rode in a square biscuit tin, while his sister had the lid.

'What can we get, that goes faster than theirs?' Vee asked her friend.

Eve thought for a while, then said: 'Hang on. I won't be long.'

She returned with her father's spade and the short-handled coal shovel. The coal shovel was the better choice. She sat on the metal scoop and steered with the handle, with her legs stretched out either side. It went like a dream and avoided any obstacles at the bottom of the slope. Vee had trouble hanging on to the heavy oak handle and fell off the spade. 'I'm going to get Mam's shovel,' Vee said.

There was a stampede of wet-nosed kids slipping and sliding back home, to raid the coal-houses. What a tournament they had that evening. Screaming and shouting brought the parents out to watch. 'Come on Beryl!' shouted Mrs. James. 'Yer can beat 'em all wi' that shiny new spade.' Beryl hit the pavement and landed in the soft deep snow, in Mrs. Morgan's front garden.

Rose and Stan came out to see their youngest child screeching and laughing as she took second place with Vee. Charlie won the race. It was times like these, on clear sky nights, when the heaven's were filled with a thousand twinkling stars, that life seemed full of hope. Rose made them all laugh by saying: 'That young Beryl is well-manured for her age.'

Stan commented: 'It's enough to make a cat laugh.'

Then her father made a bonfire out of the old sofa and some spare wood from the outhouse. Geoff poured on some petrol, siphoned from his B.S.A. bike. They roasted potatoes and chestnuts. Everyone nearby burned their rubbish that night. Metal dustbins clattered as they were tipped over the blazing fire. The folks whooping and shouting, brought out old chairs and cushions for burning. They all had a good clear out before the New Year.

Even Tilly Chapman, the old spinster, came out with brandy snaps and mince pies. Eve had overheard Jessie saying that Tilly had lost her sweetheart in The First World War. And that every night she kissed his photograph on her bedside table, waiting for his return. When Tommy was reported: Missing in Action, his parents went through the grieving process. Tilly refused to believe he'd died. His comrades said they saw him blown to bits. She still didn't give up hope, waiting for him to find her again.

Her face unmarked, with its downy white skin, belied her age. The only change was her hair, still in silky ringlets, but now white as snow. Her voice piped like a that of a coy young girl. Her virginal purity frozen in time, like the snow on the hills. She died at eighty two years old - still waiting for her lover's return.

Rose carried out a huge pan of soup and Jessie brought fresh baked bread, spread thickly with butter and strawberry jam. Every family contributed something. Eve, Vee and Charlie got hot-aches, their woolen mitten soaked through. Stan brought out tea-cloths. Warmed them in front of the fire and wrapped them round their reddened hands. It always worked.

The following morning a miserable kill-joy had strew ashes all the way down the slope. They said it must have been Snoopy Sid Braithwaite. He was the only with a car, an old Ford Popular. The kids soon found another slope. The valley was full of them.

Her father spent the next two days in the outhouse, hammering and sawing. When he finally emerged, he held a small sledge in his hands. It was made from Nan's old chiffonnier, that had stood in the outhouse since she'd first moved in with her son. Eve's sledge was inlaid with marquetry. Stan had nailed strips of steel to the curved edges. His pride and joy didn't work. The nails rusted up and prevented any good sliding action. Eve saw the disappointment in his face. 'It's fine Dad honestly...'

'Nay. Evie love. "Practice makes perfect..." I shall do better,' he replied, taking the sledge back into the outhouse. Finally the task completed, he resurfaced with his skating blades attached to the work of art. They were the type that fastened to shoes, or boots, with leather straps. Now they were strapped, nailed, screwed and soldered onto the sledge. The polished blades made it fly like the wind.

After tea Eve, Peter, Vee and David decided to go Christmas caroling to get some money, as there was a new film out called "The Purple Mask." It starred Tony Curtis and was showing at 'Highbank Pictures,' or 'The Flee Pit.' They knew from experience which of the houses to try and those to avoid. The old man at number 7 was particular hostile to kids and threw his boots at the door. Snoopy Sid never answered his door, or bought a round in the pub.

As they stood under the gas lamp in the bull-ring deciding where to go first, Vee said: 'When you and Peetrill go to college I'll be left on my own. You know I'm no good at sums, and can't spell for toffee. Reckon I'll get a job at the peanut factory.'

'You won't be lonely. We'll always be friends. It's not as if I'll be leaving home, well not until I've got some 'A' levels, or something. You can come and visit us in Italy. Anyway, we've got years left before we leave.' Vee felt sad, knowing that something important was changing and she didn't like it one bit.

'Let's go to that posh Mrs. Northorpe's house. She's really nice,' Eve said, changing the subject. They were all feeling peckish and Mrs. Northorpe made the most delicious cakes. She never gave them any money. The reward was always a cup of cocoa and a slice of cake. It was the only time the kids got chance to look inside her house. She never invited anyone indoors and always kept people talking on the door step. Near the flowered plaque on the wall that read: 'Nairobi House.'

After they'd finished one verse of: "Hark the Herald Angels Sing," the kindly lady opened the door and handed them a slice of cake each, saying: 'Stay there and I fetch you some nice hot cocoa.'

This was their chance to peep inside the hallway. The furnishing were like nothing they'd seen. Everybody had the same emerald green linoleum in their halls with a brown coconut matting runner down the middle. Rose made her daughters wrap duster round their feet and skate around on the linoleum to polish it. Many times did their father take a tumble in his work boots. But Mrs. Northorpe's carpet was Persian in deep reds and blues, resting on wood stained floor boards. And there was a mahogany table that shone under the crystal wall lights.

Nobody had wall-lights, except the picture house and the big shops in Sheffield. Everything electric trailed from a double adapter in a single light socket, in most houses. There was a china bowl on the table which had a Samuri warrior and Geisha girls, with brightly coloured flowers painted on. By the door stood a huge vase in the same design, filled with umbrellas. And the smell of something rich and aromatic filled their nostrils. Her windows never frosted up and the warmth coming from the hallway always made them feel happy and at the same time sad, because their own houses were so cold and drafty.

Mrs. Northorpe was a widow, fallen on hard times, it was said. She lived in her Council house with all the grace of the Queen Mother. Her daughter Elizabeth Rose was also very polite - and very tall. She dressed like the women in fashion magazines with tight skirts and fitted jackets. Her shoes and bags were always coordinated. She wore picture-frame hats and stepped out elegantly with a walking umbrella, which caused quite a stir on the number 19 bus. Meg had once bought such an umbrella with a long point on the end, and Eve and Vee tried so hard to copy Elizabeth Rose, but could never get the rhythm right.

It was told that Elizabeth Rose modeled for 'Vogue' magazine, in London. It must have been true because shortly after Christmas, the removal van came to their house and written on its side, it said 'Fortesque's Removals of Chelsea.' The whole street came out to nosy, and took note of every piece of antique furniture as it was carried out. There were tea-chests full of things wrapped in newspaper and huge trunks with stickers on from all over the world. They saw elephants tusks and a lion-skin rug with a stuffed head and glass eyes, carried flat to avoid it cracking. Charlie said he saw bullet holes in the back of the dead animal and all the kids gathered round to get a better look. Charlie touched its yellowed teeth and was hailed as a hero ever after.

Jessie went indoors to make a cup of tea and brought a chair out to stand on, in order to get a better view. Mrs. Northorpe hid behind the net curtains feeling exposed and uncomfortable, but Elizabeth Rose stepped out and waved to everybody, like the Queen does. Her black hair was in a French pleat and her face looked like a China doll with red rosebud lips. She was wearing Audrey Hepburn type black swagger coat with matching Capri pants and a black and white gingham checked blouse, tied at the waist. Jessie said: 'Eyup! It's the "Bluebell Girl" giving us her airs and graces.' Elizabeth had the same charm as her mother so nobody was offended.

Finally when Mrs. Northorpe came out of hibernation, Rose and Jessie went to kiss her and wish her luck. Both of them a little envious of her leaving the grime filled valley. Jessie asked her if she intended to take the net curtains, and if not, could she have them. Elizabeth Rose went back inside and brought them out, still on the wires, for Jessie. For the first time the folks could see inside the sitting room and were amazed by the velvet flocked wallpaper with gold stripes.

As the van departed with the kids running behind it, the folks raided the garden. Stripped it bare of every rosebush and tree they could dig up. No one managed to prize out the lilac tree and it continued to flower long after Mrs. Northorpe and Elizabeth Rose left. 'A little keepsake', Jessie said, as she replanted three rose bushes in the freezing hard ground of her back garden.

When the light disappeared the Carol singers had gathered

enough coppers to get them into the cinema. The lamp lighter reached up to the glass lantern with his long pole and turned on the gas, then lit the wick on one of the remaining few gas lamps, scattered along the older section of the village. His days were numbered. Electric street lighting had arrived in Blackridge.

The plan was for Charlie to sneak under the counter hoping the dopey, short-sighted old woman, who also doubled as usherette, wouldn't get up quick enough to see him in the dark. Peter blew onto the cold glass that separated the old woman from would be attackers, asking for three 'Halves.' Peering through the steamed up window she never saw how many cinema-goers were out there. She didn't care. This way the "Four Musketeers" would have enough for an ice-cream during the interval and a little over for chips on the way home. They only hoped that 'Beefie,' the manager was around, or they'd all get a wolloping with his rubber torch.

Walking back in the dim glow thrown from the gas lamps, sharing a large 6d bag of fish scraps and chips, Vee started to feel isolated again, knowing her friends would take exams she couldn't possibly pass. She dreamed of being whisked away by "The Purple Mask," until she met the new landlord's son Donald Pinder.

Relight My Fire

Donnie and his parents lived above "The Blacksmith's Arms." His father was a heavy drinker and enjoyed the buzz of pub life, while Donnie despised alcohol and drank nothing but ice-cream soda and Vimto.

It was a hot summer's night when Vee first set eyes on Donnie. She was fourteen and had dressed up to go with her parents down to the pub. Of course Charlie came along too. They sat outside in the garden at the back and played on the swings until 10p.m. in the evening, watching the sun go down over the factories. Sparks and grinding noises from the smelting forge behind the pub, lit up the darkening sky. Jessie's curls clung desperately to her head then started to wilt at sunset. As she and Johnny munched their crisps, her large false teeth clattering, Vee spotted a slim fair-haired lad taking photos of her.

'What do you think you're doing?' she shouted, running over to him.

'Well you looked so lovely sitting there with the sunset behind you. It made your hair turn into a nut brown colour,' he said, shyly.

For the first time in her life Vee was lost for words. She thought the quiet lad looked like James Dean in the film "East of Eden". This first simple childlike observation was to prove more accurate than she realized. 'Would you like me to show you how I develop and print the films? My dark room's in the cellar.'

'Is that so?' said Vee, regaining her composure. 'Well all right then, but NO funny business!'

'I wouldn't dream of it,' he said, earnestly.

Vee looked disappointed. She wanted to be kissed. She had this aching to be kissed. She ended up making a move on him in the red gloom as they watched the ghost-like images slowly appearing in the trays, kissing him until he couldn't breathe, then left shouting: 'See Ya!'

Donnie followed her around like a lamb after that, and thinking to impress her persuaded his Dad to buy an American car. It was silver blue and fluorescent pink, with massive chrome bumpers, a loud horn - and a radio. As Vee walked home from school with Eve, Peter and Charlie, they were followed by this huge machine chugging and back-firing behind them, with Donnie staring over the chrome steering wheel, windows down and music blaring out. Before they reached Vee's house the car stalled and shuddered to a stop.

Later Vee found out that if Donnie drove her round the block a gallon of petrol would be guzzled up. She didn't care. She had a boyfriend who looked like James Dean, with a car, who thought she was beautiful.

'Mam!' she announced, 'I'm going to marry Donnie Pinder when I'm sixteen and he's got a right big Chevy!'

Donnie's generosity of spirit endeared him to Vee's friends and their families. Nothing was too much trouble. He'd pick them up from school, spending all his allowance on petrol. He taught all of them how to develop and print and would lend his expensive camera to Peter anytime. Donnie was glad to be alive, with friends of his own at last, engaged to a girl who made his heart sing - and to be away from his volatile father and the pub as much as possible.

The "Five Musketeers" became inseparable and did everything together. While Vee and Donnie snogged heavily in the front seat, Peter and Eve sat in the back and talked of what they would do when they got to Italy, with Charlie in the middle of them, turning the pages of the book on "The Uffizi."

∽

After Anton left, Eve made herself a cup of coffee and lit up a cigarette. She decided to give smoking up for the New Year. As is the way with human nature, being poor again she needed to smoke more than ever. Heathcliffe was found in Anton's shed, curled in a ball on the deck chair, so she handed over the cat food and biscuits to her friend. Thinking now was as good as ever to make the break. It was as if the mad cat knew it was time to leave the sinking ship, after all the rat had gone first.

The recliner didn't look as inviting anymore without the challenge. It just stood there, very old and battered with the stuffing hanging out. She understood the feeling. Like all cats, Heathcliffe had ignored the scratching post and used the furniture instead. 'Bonfire time!' The canvasses tied together in the hall reflected her half-hearted attempts at Impressionistic painting. She dragged the old chair outside to the garden, put the canvasses on top, doused them with petrol and threw in a match. 'That feels good!' she said, warming her hands near the flames. Catharsis completed. Curls of black smoke snaked up into the cold night air. 'Good riddance to bad rubbish!' she said, walking back into the house.

She didn't take the rare French Baccarat millifiori paperweight out of the box, so she never saw the tiny butterfly poised for flight in the central cane. She already knew what she'd lost. Her whole pre-soon-to-be-ex life was spent dreaming of painting in Italy. If only she'd shown the dome to Peter, then, maybe, something better would have happened. Maybe he would have read the meaning in the paperweight. It was too late now to change things. "You make your bed you lie in it!" her father's voice echoed in her ear.

She tried to take stock of her life with the husband, wondering where the years had gone. Why had they stayed together? Her every evening became predictable. The days drift into years. One funeral after another. Old Gran and the husband getting more and more somber with each bereavement. Then it dawned on her she'd spent her whole life dreaming of a better future. She knew from experience that the old folks longed for the past. Better days. Don't know what's happening to the world, they'd say. All these years she'd not savored the moment. They way children did naturally. She saved for a rainy day, when there would be pennies from heaven. Just leave it Dad, she said, as these thoughts came into her head.

After she and the husband moved from the Funeral Parlour things got a little better. She read a lot and chatted to the neighbours. The husband always came home late. At least he wasn't dealing in death. She hoped college would improve his humour. He read Shakespeare and Chaucer as well as Flashman and the Beano. When she got home from work she threw herself into keeping fit. Stopped herself thinking about the miserable life she led. Went for

Jane Fonda's 'burn', yoga, aerobics, weight-training, jogging and swimming. Became athletic and svelte again in her mid Thirties, until she damaged the cartilage in her knee.

It didn't happen while going for the burn. Nothing as glamorous as that. One night, about 11.00p.m. she needed to go for a pee. In sliding her right leg out from under the duvet a mere fraction, her leg locked. It was the most agonizing pain. She couldn't move. The husband hadn't returned from the Snooker Hall. Fortunately there was a phone by the bed. Not wanting to disturb her neighbours, and ready to pass out any time, she called for an ambulance.

When the ambulance arrived fifteen minutes later, she managed to hop over to the window and throw down the door keys, from her hand bag. Mitch had the habit of pinching her cigarettes and the odd note from her purse, so she kept the bag in the bedside cupboard. When they got up to the bedroom she was lying on the floor moaning softly.

'Now lass. What's the problem?' Dave asked.

'I can't bend my knee...it's agony,' she groaned.

'Lift her onto the bed Malcom,' he said to his mate. 'We'll have to strap it up love.'

While Dave swathed the whole of her leg in tight wadding, Malcom went for the stretcher.

'Can't I shuffle down the stairs on my bottom?' she pleaded. Dave hadn't exactly got the delicate touch - and the staircase was extremely narrow.

'Wouldn't hear of it,' he said.

After the two men had strapped her into the stretcher, it looked like something from a mountain rescue. The thing must have measured somewhere in the region of eight feet long, including poles. Dave was a foot taller than Malcom. She was pouring with sweat from the pain. The ascent was imminent.

'Righto Malcom you take it steady through the door, then try and get round onto the landing.'

Malcom struggled in the lead and wedged the stretcher in the doorway. 'Bloody-well back up a bit,' he cursed, then seeing Eve's face added: 'We'll soon have you in the ambulance love. We've got gas and air for the pain.'

After ten minutes of crashing into the handrail and reversing into the hot-water tank cupboard they put her down for a rest, before tackling the bend on the stairs.

'WHAT YOU BE DOING UP THERE?...You being all right luff?'

It was Anton. She didn't know whether to laugh or cry.

'Let me be coming past. Moving out of way... What you be doing to yourself luff. Has bastard been hurting you?'

She explained to him what had happened, then threw up all over the stretcher. The two red-faced ambulance men exhaled and shrugged their shoulders. Anton gave her the toilet roll and they took up the poles again.

'Please don't drop me,' she wailed, unable to move and feeling helpless in the straight jacket. Now she understood why gangsters knee-capped their enemies. Maximum pain. She managed to free an arm and tried to wipe the sick out of her hair.

They slid the stretcher over the handrail and Dave clung on to the poles as she was lowered over the stairs. Then Anton took a stance under the middle of the stretcher. He took the full weight until the two amigos found their bearings. She could feel his head and hands supporting her backside. 'Now be moving forward. Slowly... One and two...One and two...' He counted them down each step, like a drill seargant. Each step jarred her knee. She dripped sweat from her head, groaning with every movement.

Finally they arrived at the ambulance door. Anton locked the front door and hopped in beside her. 'I be coming with you luff. You being all right now?' She sucked in the gas and air greedily, until she felt dizzy, as the ambulance sped away.

'Put the siren on Dave,' Malcom shouted to his mate. 'It'll relieve the tension...I had my cartilage taken out, you know,' he shouted above the siren. 'Terrible pain, it was. Agonizing...Massive scarring. On crutches for six month. I've limped ever since. It'll never be right. Arthritis develops, then the joints wear away,' he sighed. 'Bone grinding on bone... Crunch! Crunch! You can hear it when I walk...' He clicked his knee back and forth to demonstrate. 'There's nothing they can do. Artificial knee replacements don't last long - if you can get one on NHS...I'll probably end up in a wheel chair,' he added, rubbing his knee.

Before they got to the hospital, they had another pick up. An unconscious drunken tramp who had filled his pants. They slid him along the pavement, leaving a snail's trail of poo behind. Then heaved him onto the ambulance floor, between Eve and Anton.

For once Anton didn't cause a fuss, because he'd shared the gas and air with Eve. By the time they got to the hospital they were both giggling like children. The tramp was dragged out of the ambulance and left in the hospital foyer. Then Dave swilled the inside of the vehicle with Dettol and boiling water. The exhausted night-shift doctor gave her some strong pain killers and asked her to return on Monday for an X-Ray. With luck the cartilage might slip back in again. It didn't. When Monday arrived her leg had ballooned. She had the torn cartilage cut out on Wednesday. While disabled for three months, she took up knitting and managed to complete the back and front of a jumper for the husband. When the pattern got to the sleeves she gave up and binned it.

She decided to have it out with the husband. Confirm her suspicions. Had he got another woman? He denied everything. In the meantime his golf partner, Jonathon, covered for his infidelities. It was Dora, Jonathon's wife, who completely cocked up his alibi. The husband told Eve he'd stayed at Jonathon's house after late night drinking. He and Jonathon had supposedly celebrated the end of term in style. He was too drunk to drive. Dora said they'd been away for the weekend, to visit her mother in Carlisle.

On the positive side, she had time to deal with the problem. She didn't have to face her work mates with swollen eyes. She could be as miserable as she wanted, without anyone criticizing. Bawl her eyes out, and nobody would say: 'Keep your chin up...The world's your oyster...Smile though your heart is breaking.' Low key and private, she thought. Mavis and Shirl couldn't embellish what they hadn't heard. They invented instead.

She felt relieved when turning the last page of "Lord of the Rings," then went back to enjoying D.H. Lawrence's Short Stories and Emily Dickinson's poetry. Mitch showed a little concern. He told her to leave the vacuuming, until she recovered. Anton did her shopping and cleaning. During her incapacitation, one night when Mitch came home early she asked him to teach her Poker. It seemed the house would never be sold. An endless round of prospective purchasers, coming and going, looking down their noses. Wondering why she was on crutches.

He became more civil. Almost nice. Wanted to work it out. She decided to keep things as normal as possible. Try again. Take an interest in at least one of his hobbies. Something to pass the time. Also she was desperate for companionship. She needed more human interaction. Golf would cost him money, and she was in no fit state to stand, let alone swing a club.

Divorce proceedings were put on hold. Then the Jackson family decided they wanted the house. The husband said they should continue with the sale. Make a fresh start. Buy a new house at a later date. She felt weary. Went along with his suggestion. Her knee ached all the time and her elbows became sore from hoisting herself backwards up the stairs. The weight piled on.

Thus the marathon games commenced. At first they played for pegs, until she became quite proficient and won the whole bag. Mitch, a fervent gambler, decided on the new stakes. The list read: making coffee for a week, cleaning the car, washing up, ironing, decorating, cleaning windows. He not done any of these chores before. And now he had no intention of doing them after. Confidant in his prowess. He lost game after game because she became good at bluffing. Showing excitement when she held a lousy hand and looking disappointed with four Aces. Confused him. For a while he forgot about Miss Whiplash. She took second place, as the gambling fever grew in him. Took up the gauntlet. They played for money, until she got a Running Flush and cleared his wallet. He fumed and sulked unable to accept defeat, so she gave him the money back. Slammed doors were difficult to open on crutches. At least he spent more time at home, she thought.

Then he bought: a Chess Set, Backgammon, Trivial Pursuit, Scrabble, Monopoly and even Ludo. Before she could take her coat off, and set down her crutches, on returning from Physiotherapy, he'd set up the games. Her mates Dave and Malcom took her there and back every afternoon, for her treatment. A daily trip to the decrepit building way out in the sticks, was her link with civilization.

Meanwhile Mitch became increasingly desperate to win. No

matter what. They played for cigarettes and chores. For weeks she waited for the chores to be done, while he smoked her winnings, after she'd gone to bed. When the fever finally abated and the marathon games ended, he had welched on all bets.

His complete withdrawal occurred after their failed attempts at camaraderie. Not a word was spoken thereafter. He stayed out later than usual and slept in the spare room. She had compounded his destruction, by finishing his unsolved Solitaire game, just after winning at Snakes and Ladders and before making the coffee. Maybe she should have let him win sometimes, she thought. Arm-wrestling? Line-dancing? Long jump? She didn't and couldn't. It was her way of paying him back for years of disrespect.

He won in the end though, because he knew she couldn't sleep until he arrived home. Sometimes it was as late as 4.0a.m. when he crashed into the spare bed. Miss Whiplash had worn him out. Eve revisited her solicitor in a taxi, with the aid of a walking stick.

Rescue Me

It happened just before Vee and Donnie were due to marry. Donnie had asked his Dad for some money for a deposit on a house. It wasn't a large sum - and almost nothing to the wealthy pub owner.

'Why can't you live here, as always. You know all this will be yours when I'm gone.'

'I ddon't want to live in a ppub anymore,' he stuttered, fearful of his father's temper.

'Not good enough for you now, is it?'

'It's not that ddad...1 just wwant a fresh start.'

'Fresh start is it, well, you can pack your bags now Sonny Jim. Go on! Bugger off and don't come back. Ungrateful bleeder, there'll be no more money from me,' he shouted, pushing his son to the door.

His mother came downstairs. 'What's to do George? Leave the poor lad alone. Haven't you knocked him about enough. Pick on someone your own size,' she said, standing up to him, to save her son from a beating. Without a second thought George Pinder punched his wife in the face, knocking her to the floor.

For the first time in his life Donnie felt rage instead of fear, right in the pit of his stomach, like a ball of fire that was about to explode. 'LEAVE HER ALONE!' he shouted, when George went to kick his wife. Donnie tried to help his mother up, turning his back on his father. The next thing he felt was an agonizing pain, as a bottle smashed over his head. With blood gushing down his face he staggered from the blow.

'Stop it please!' his mother begged.

Donnie charged at his father knocking the wind out of him. He was twice the size of his son, but had drunk a bottle of whisky already, so he stumbled into the bar. Then Donnie did something totally alien to his nature. He swung his fist right up into his father's jaw. It connected and knocked him senseless.

'You'd best leave son, before he sobers up,' his mother said softly, pulling herself up.

'What about you Ma? Haven't you had enough being his punch bag?'

'He doesn't know what he's doing love. Anyway how would he managed on his own? He'd just drink himself into an early grave. At least this way he'll stay sober for a week or so.'

She took a handful of notes from the till and pressed them to him. 'Nay Ma! It's just blood money!' He kissed her and went out to the car.

Rose had persuaded Jessie to try out the new hairdressers in the village. It would be a trial run before the wedding. Maureen was taking on customers for the new permanent waving process. Jessie reluctantly took out her curlers, mid week, feeling self conscious and walked to the salon. When she saw the contraptions inside, she turned on her heels and walked back out. 'Now! Now! Jessie. Come on love. It won't hurt one bit,' said Rose, taking her arm and leading her back.

All round the edges of the salon were hair-dryers that looked more like atomic bombs, except they were coloured pink and right in the centre was Maureen's pride and joy, something straight out of Frankenstein.

'What the bloody hell is that?' said Jessie, standing back in fear. 'It my new perming machine,' Maureen said, smiling. 'Now come on Mrs. Buttersworth. There's nothing to be scared of. Let Susan there, wash your hair first.'

Jessie reluctantly sat in the chair and folded her arms, while her friend smiled reassuringly, sitting beside her. 'How I'm supposed to get me head over the bowl?'

'It's a backwards wash Mrs. Butterworth,'

'What?'

Rose put a towel round her own shoulders to demonstrate and leaned back for Beryl to do the honours.

After Jessie was washed and towel dried, Maureen lopped off

six inches of hair and started the lengthy procedure of solution/paper/curler, until Jessie felt quite a home, apart from the foul stink coming from the lotion. She had a long roll of cotton wool draped round her forehead over her ears and fixed at the back, to stop the solution running down and burning her face. What Jessie didn't know what that she was going to be wired up.

An hour later the rollers were fully connected to the cables above and Jessie was earthed to the chair. Her mouth opened as Maureen switched on, shouting: 'Welcome to Blackpool Illuminations.' Jessie vowed at that moment, if she lived through it, never to visit a hairdresser ever again. Not that she had ever been to one before.

The rollers eventually came out, after drying, rinsing, washing, rising and drying again and Jessie had a mass of little lamb's tail curls. Her dark brown straight hair had been transformed by this miracle of science - and at the same time lightened two shades. She didn't notice that the ends were like straw, or the strange yellowish tinge, because at last she was curler free. A good night's sleep for the first time in years was imminent.

Maureen scooped out a dollop of Brylcream and massaged it into the dead ends. From that moment on Jessie's life was changed. She looked in the mirror and smiled a gummy smile, saying: 'Eat your bloody heart out Rita Hayworth!'

The afternoon ended with fish and chips and a glass of shandy at "The Blacksmith's Arms" and even Rose had a tipple, relieved that Jessie was happy with her lot. Jessie chattered happily about the forthcoming wedding and how she'd persuaded the vicar to play a record of wedding bell sounds through the microphone, as the chapel didn't have a belfry. Donnie's mother came to them outside.

'What on earth has happened to you lass?' Jessie asked, looking at her swollen face.

'Oh. It's nothing,' she said, covering her cheek. 'I've got some bad news, I'm afraid. We've just heard our Donnie's had a crash. I'm off to the hospital now. Can't stop, there's a taxi waiting outside.'

'How is he? Is he all right!' said Jessie, starting to panic.

'He's in a bad way they say... Got to go now...Find Vee.'

Donnie put his foot flat to the floor, racing along the narrow lanes, satiating his anger, hedgerows and fences becoming a blur. He tried to avoid the dog. It was black and white, only slightly bigger than a pup. It just ran out in front of the car. There was nothing he could do but step on the brakes. Then there was a dull thud of the car hitting the dog and the feeling of it being dragged under the wheels - and his own body smashing through the windscreen. The dog didn't yelp or make a sound but died instantly. And himself, sailing through the air as if he had wings. He didn't remember the falling, or the impact, only flying like an angel - and the soft tinkling of glass.

Vee arrived at the hospital to find Donnie swathed in bandages. His face swollen to twice its normal size and both his eyes purple and closed. A neck and shoulder brace covered in plaster, kept his broken arm and fractured collar bone supported. His face has suffered the most damage and was badly scarred from the razor sharp glass. 'Donnie? ...It's me....Don't worry. I'll stay with you all night... You'll soon be better... It'll be all right love.'

He tried to speak, but was unable to because of the stitches and the swelling. She'd been told by the surgeon that he would be scarred for life -and she knew what he was thinking.

'Donnie Pinder!' she shouted, tears streaming down her face. 'You've got to get better. I can't managed without you... We're getting married in six weeks time come hell or high water... and... I... I love you!' He attempted a smile. No one had ever told him that before.

Move Closer

30th December.

Anton stayed away. Eve hadn't seen him all day. Walking round to his front door, she knocked loudly, hoping he was all right. 'Anton! Are you in,' she shouted through the letter box. 'It's Eve... I brought you a jam and cream donut... Your favourite.' She heard shuffling and then the door was unlocked. Anton's eyes were red and he looked upset.

'What's wrong,' she asked, half knowing.

'I'm being very sorry luff. I spoiling your future chances now you not getting any money.'

'Anton,' she said seriously. 'It was totally my doing and, believe me, it was worth every penny to see him drive away sat in cat poo! Now are you going to keep me standing out here for ever. It's freezing!'

He chuckled and said, 'Be coming in luff and wiping feet.' Then he pointed towards the sitting room. 'I crying eyes out luff, last night, and mad cat he be knowing about this. Ever since luff, he not be letting me out of his sight.'

She looked into the sitting room and saw Heathcliffe ensconced in the best armchair, growling softly at her. Anton chattered for a while, mainly talking about Maudie, then asked: 'Why you be marrying pillock like him. Why you no be marrying good man... Have you ever been loving anyone else better luff?'

'There was this boy once. Peter Hill but we were such good friends that any thoughts of romance were kept hidden because I didn't want to spoil things. Then the Soon-to-be-ex turned up!'

'Bastard! ... Telling me luff how you be meeting him.'

'It was my Sixteenth birthday and most of the villagers had arranged a special party for me and Vee and Donnie, my friends. They didn't have a proper wedding reception as Donnie was involved in a serious crash. He managed to walk his new wife back down the aisle though.'

❧

Eve thought back to the day of the party. She had gone to see Mrs. Pinkerton earlier than usual. She'd not been to the Fairground for three years and wanted to tell the kind woman about her plans for Italy. 'Hello! Flame-haired girl. Long time no see.' She was setting up the stall and dressed in white satin with black polka dots.

'Hello Mrs. Pinkerton. I'm so glad to see you. I thought perhaps you wouldn't be here.'

'I'll be here until Seven. Now child I have two for the price of one magical paperweights just for you. One has a white rose in the centre and if you give it a good shake the snow falls. The other is amber glass, nothing much. No need to look at it unless you really need to. For you special price, one shilling for both.'

She handed over the money and gave Mrs. Pinkerton a little gift wrapped in Christmas paper. It was a second-hand silver cigarette case.

'Just to thank you for your encouragement and advice,' she said. 'Peter, 'the blue eyed boy' and I are going to Italy in two years time. It's all planned.'

'Child! Heed my warning! Before you go out tonight make sure you give this dome a good shake. It's very important,' she said, staring at the paperweight. 'And give this ointment to your friend with the scars on his face. It will help them fade.'

Eve usually believed what Mrs. Pinkerton said at the time, but afterwards didn't really give much thought to her warnings, thinking they were merely coincidence. But this last statement made her eyes open wide.

'How do you know...'

'My child, I know many things. Now go enjoy your birthday... Remember...'

The house was full of excitement as they all got ready for the party. It was to be held the church hall. A band had been organized 'Billie Biddle and his Cheeky Chappies', a motley crew, all over seventy, but cheap. Jessie, Rose and Meg had organized the food and Johnny had arranged for some beer barrels to be delivered.

'Keith and I are going to practice our 'Quick Step' upstairs. Won't be long,' Angela announced.

Eve followed them up knowing that Angela would use her room. She quickly cleared her dressing table of all breakables, putting the paperweight in the bottom drawer with the others, intending to retrieve it later. As they bounced up and down on the floor boards, all the girls downstairs were slapping on their make up.

There was Vee and Vivian, Eve and Meg, Jessie and Rose. Of course Vivian had the largest, most perfect beehive hairdo, sprayed with pink to match her dress.

'They'll bloody well be coming through the floor boards,' Jessie said, as Angela and Keith thundered around upstairs.

'Well that's our Angela for you, always one to make a grand entrance,' Rose replied laughing.

Then she set out the rest of the food in carrier bags, to be taken to the Church Hall, putting one bag aside containing party hats and streamers, for June Smith and the girls. She had been invited to the party but was now too ill to go out in the cold weather.

'Well, you can't see the babbies go hungry, can you?' she said to Jessie. 'Don't forget Meg love, drop it off on your way.'

Eve had on her first tight fitting dress. It was emerald green satin with a square neck. She had found some satin high heels to match and a little mock tiara with dark green stones, like emeralds only paste. At last she was ready for her naming, just like Meg and Angela had been named after a film star.

'Our Evie you look beautiful,' her mother said. 'Doesn't she Stan?'

'Lovely,' he said, smiling.

'Well Dad... What about my name then?' she asked him, nervously.

'Our Little Evie, don't you know your own name.'

'She means her Film Star name Stan,' Rose whispered to him.

He remained silent and in this silence Eve decided, there and then, that her father didn't think her pretty enough to be a film star.

'You look like Greer Garson,' her mother quickly said.

Angela stood at the door, and looking Eve up and down said: 'She an old fogie, isn't she?'

'Greer Garson is the most beautiful woman on the pictures, so just shut it!'

And that was that. She couldn't move into that mysterious world of womanhood, as her sisters had done with such ease - not without a Film Star name from her father.

Stan couldn't believe how his 'Little One' had grown up so quickly. He felt as if he was losing her, the child he treasured for her gentleness and patience, who always told him how much she loved him. The one who looked most like his beloved Rose. He knew he had to let go some time, but not right at that moment. She wouldn't marry for ages. Got her head screwed on right. College girl. He breathed a sigh of relief and fastened his tie.

As the three sister set off for the party arm in arm, with the birthday girl in the middle. Angela said, 'Come on then "Bucket Chops," let's see if we can get you fixed up tonight. You don't want to be an old maid, do you!' Eve felt an overwhelming love for both her sisters at that moment. She would soon be a woman and join them in their world. After she and Peter had toured Italy.

Instead of going straight to the church hall Angela insisted they had a drink in the pub first.

'Not for me thanks, just an orange juice,' said Meg as Keith came over from the bar.

'I'll have a Barley Wine and get one for our Evie. It's time she let go a bit.'

'She's underage Angela,' Meg whispered.

'What the eye doesn't see...' she said laughing. 'You'll love it Evie!'

Eve took her first mouthful of alcohol and grimaced. 'It's horrible!' she said.

'Try a big gulp and you'll feel much better,' Angela urged. Eve did as she was told. Tonight she felt especially nervous and she needed a little confidence, as she was going to make a speech for Vee and Donnie - and tell Peter that she loved him.

'I'm going then Evie. Be careful... Geoff's Mum will be having trouble settling the twins. They're so excited. We've got to put out a mince pie and a glass of sherry for Santa. David says he wants to leave a carrot for Rudolph but Daniel says he'll like Christmas cake better... Don't be long Angela! Mum will need some help putting the food out... See you later alligator.'

'Not for a while crocodile,' Angela drawled, rolling her eyes.

After her third Barley Wine on an empty stomach Eve was nearly on the floor. Her tongue felt too big for her mouth, so when she tried to speak it sounded really weird. Angela thought it was hysterical, until Keith intervened.

'Come on love. Let's get you out in the fresh air,' he said lifting Eve up and holding onto her arm. The fresh air made matters worse. Eve felt dizzy and sick and her legs wouldn't go where she wanted them to go.

They finally reached the Church Hall and steered Eve over to a chair, as far away from her mother as possible. Fortunately the hall was starting to fill up so she wasn't so noticeable, slouching in the chair. Her face almost the same colour as the dress.

Peter was standing awkwardly at the other side of the large hall holding a single white rose. He was just about to try and reach Eve when the band burst in, cursing loudly.

'That bloody pillock in the hearse nearly killed us! We're lucky to be here, I can tell you!' exclaimed Billy, his sludge brown wig falling to one side. 'We were just coming over the pass along that narrow bit with the long ditch, when this daft fart in a hearse, of all bloody things, decides to overtake. Charra nearly went over the edge... Gives us a pint quick!'

Everyone milled round to hear the story again. Then the band set up on the stage. Billie played drums and bongos, Fred on guitar and trombone, Cyril thwacked the double base and throttled the trumpet, Harry on piano -and spoons if requested.

'Ladies and gentlemen take your partners for a slow fox-trot.'

The music started, wavering at first then speeding up into any rhythm they could manage, usually three four time. At least they all finished together, but got worse as the night went on. Folk didn't mind, it was a change to have live music - if you could call it that, with Cyril leaning on his double base looking ready to drop anytime.

Peter had been encouraged by his family to finally tell Eve his real feelings, hoping she was in the same state of mind. His mother had taught him how to waltz and his father had bought him a new suit. Jessie, Rose, and Eileen Hill stood at the food table, giving Peter the nod to get over to Eve as soon as possible. None of them knew how ill she was feeling as she had slouched even further down in the chair and was ready to slide onto the floor.

It was hard for him to get through the mass of villagers shuffling round the dance floor and the music was so loud he decided to wait. In that moment of hesitation his future was to change for the worse, as a lanky spotty lad, with his trousers at half mast came in through the fire exit door.

He had parked the hearse round the back in the dark, thinking that if he got lucky tonight, it would look like a large saloon car from the front angle. He hadn't intended to spend Christmas Eve out in the sticks, but got lost following some old codgers in a clapped out coach, thinking they were heading for Sheffield.

The first person he saw, as he sneaked into the hall trying to avoid the band, was a young raver slouching in a chair and drunk as a lord.

'Do you want to come outside?' he asked in his slickest voice.

'Oh! God! Yes!'

He couldn't believe his luck.

Eve staggered toward the fire exit, burst through the doors like Billy the Kid and threw up over the bonnet of the hearse. Now most young men would have been disgusted, but not Mitcham Robert Crookshank. He thought it was great and that she must be a really fast bird.

Fortunately for Eve, her sister Meg and Geoff came bursting through the fire doors, followed by Rose and Stan, then Jessie and Johnny and finally, Vee and Donnie. Angela stayed well out of the way.

What's this? The posse? he thought, or worse, a lynch mob.

'I've not touched her!' he pleaded. They ignored him.

'Wait till I get my hands on our Angela!' Rose said. 'Evie love?

It's me, your mother? Are you all right?... Stand back, give her some air!'

Eve wretched again until there was nothing left.

'Mum! I've gone blind. I can't see!' she cried, as the car park started to spin. The lone charrabang and hearse whizzing round made her think she was going crazy. 'Mum! I can see a hearse! Help me!'

'Come on now Evie let's get you home lass,' Jessie said, handing her a glass of water.

'She's not fit to walk. Has anyone else got a car? The band's three sheets to the wind,' Johnny said, then noticed the big black saloon covered in sick. 'Is that yours mate?'

Mitch nodded, sheepishly. All he wanted to do was get out of this place alive.

'Here pal!' Geoff said, handing him the fire bucket full of water. 'Rinse it down and give the family a lift home, will you?'

Geoff was a man of few words, but stocky in build after boxing for the Navy, so people tended to listen when he did speak. And Mitch being a born coward took the bucket of water, threw it over the bonnet and asked them all to climb inside the car.

'Well! I'll go to the foot of our stairs - It's a bloody hearse! I'm not getting in that!' said Jessie.

'It's all right Jessie. We'll manage. You go inside and enjoy the party.'

So Rose, Meg and Eve in the front seat along with poor Stan, Geoff, Vee and Donnie in the back, looking very nervous leaning against the glass windows, were taken back to number 23. The silence only broken by Eve moaning and saying, 'Let me die Mum!'

༼ঌ

'You see Anton, Mitch came into my life and rescued me, as least I thought so at the time - unfortunately.'

Eve had got her wires crossed again and believed that Peter hadn't bothered to help her in her hour of need because he felt disgusted by her behaviour, when in fact, he'd seen a spotty youth taking her outside; giving him a wink and the thumbs up! His father saying in the background, 'Looks like you've missed the boat lad!'

ARMY DREAMER

30th December.

Anton invited Eve round for dinner that evening, as an appeasement. 'I cooking proper Polish dish with lamb and herbs. Wanting to be coming round luff?'

'Course I do. I'll get a good bottle of Claret and a lemon tart for pudding. We'll push the boat out on the night before New Year's Eve.'

He enjoyed having Eve round for meals. She reminded him of Maudie. Always kind. Never complained. She was a good listener. Somehow just by her being there helped him forget. His much loved Maudie. She had comforted. The one who held him, when he awoke in the night crying out. The woman who calmed his anger and frustration. Love at first sight, for him. She took more persuasion. She walked out with Janek Baryla first. He was educated. Spoke good English. Anton liked him. It was a difficult decision. In the end his heart won.

Anton and Janek worked in the factory. They had the worst job. Back breaking labour. Feckling the pipes was a task nobody wanted. They gave it to the Poles instead. Janek was calmer than Anton. A man of reason. He laughed when the workers called him: 'Jam Roll.' He took it in his stride. Not Anton.

'Why you be calling me Jam Roll?'

'Jam Roll - Pole!' laughed Sid, in the Smelting Shop.

'You be taking it back!' Anton said, getting hot under the collar.

Janek tried to pull him away. Sid stood six feet tall in his work boots, with a girth to match. Anton was a mere 5'3".

'You be insulting my honour and my country. You taking it back, I saying!'

'Come on lads. Let it lie,' Bert said, trying to smooth things over.

'This little bastard thinks he can take me on... So come on... let's see what you're made of JAM ROLL!' Before he could speak another word, Anton leaped up and punched him right in the mouth. Then he started dancing round, fists at the ready. Marquis of Queensbury style.

'Come on yourself bastard! My name is Anton Morawksi. ANTON MORAWSKI! You hearing it? Be listening good pillock... Polish winter not be killing me! Starvation making me want to live... Germans not be finishing me off. Let me be seeing you trying FAT CHUFFING!'

The workers encircled the two opponents, waiting for the slaughter. Sid had a vile temper. He stood and wiped the blood from his mouth. Spat out a tooth. Then he smiled. 'Put it here, Anton Morawski. You're O.K. in my book.' Sid held out his fat hairy hand and Anton glared at him.

'Not before you apologizing to me and my friend!' Anton had fists at the ready.

A sharp intake of breath from the men. Sid put his hands on his hips, threw his head back and laughed out loud.

Anton was just about to wallop him again, when Sid replied: 'I apologize to you, Anton...and to you Janek...Now will you shake on it?'

Anton nodded. Strutted over and took the big man by the hand. Then he turned and pointed at the workers, saying: 'If any of you EVER be calling me Jam Roll again, I KILLING YOU! O.K?'

They nodded. No one ever used the derogatory term again. He'd won their respect - and learned to curse as good as the rest of them.

Shortly after this event Anton and Janek fell out. Anton not one to hang back, told Maudie simply and plainly he was going to marry her. She ignored him. He followed Janek and Maudie around, like a lost soul. He was devastated by the rejection. He didn't have a good enough grasp of English to write love letters. Janek wrote fluently. He became tongue-tied while Janek articulated. His heart bursting with love. But it was Janek who held her gloved hand. Anton had no way to declare his honourable intentions.

Then one day as she walked through the park, he sang. Sang as if his life depended upon it. Everyone around stopped and listened to his clear voice, as it carried from the Band Stand. They were mesmerized. 'O Sole Mio.' He'd learned the Italian words. The handsome young man with his hair plastered down. Wearing his best suit and holding a bunch of heather he'd picked from the moors. He stirred her heart. There was something melancholic, deeply moving even, about the way he sang. He touched her with his emotional rendition.

Poor Janek was pushed out into the cold. He never forgave Anton for stealing his girlfriend. Not until Maudie's death did the two men speak again, even though their paths crossed every day. A quick handshake and a nod, meant all was forgiven.

The food Anton cooked for dinner tasted delicious. Heathcliffe chewed on a plate of lamb in the kitchen, minced up finely for the old mog. 'You wanting a brandy luff?'

'No thanks. I'm fine with my coffee.'

'I getting good video to be watching: "The Godfather."'

Moving into the sitting room, Eve said she'd prefer one of his stories.

'Tell me more about your life in Poland, when you moved up into the mountains.'

Anton looked serious and began:

'We living up in mountains, as you knowing. After Grandmother dying, father dying year after with T.B. It being too cold up there and killing many people. Very bad winter...My mother she nursing him through illness. She delivering many babies and taking care of sick people. They calling her 'Angel'. I being only fourteen years old then - and man of the house. My sisters and me working, working, working, all day. Cutting trees, catching rabbits, fixing things, doing jobs, anything for food. A few chickens for special occasions, when wolves not be getting them. Then the Germans coming to Poland... Bastards! We thinking we being safe up in mountains.

Friends down in village, who my mother be helping, warning us about shop keeper being informer. I not telling you this before but my Grandparents being full Romany gypsies. My mother she is marrying father, he is Catholic and we being Catholic also, as you know luff.

One night the soldiers coming up mountain... They taking mother and sisters... dragging them screaming, screaming luff! I trying to stop them... I trying my best but they kicking me and beating. I trying to getting up but they kicking and kicking me. I could not be doing nothing luff...'

❧

That fine crisp day up in the mountains Anton and his sisters sang as they worked. The family was better off now. Grandmother had provided for them, in anticipation of her death. A horse and cart enabled him to sell logs in the village and bring supplies back more easily. There were rabbits hanging in the larder, the chickens had produced eggs and the smell of baking came from the house that used to belong to his Grandmother.

Anton loved living up the mountains. The air was fresh, and he felt as if the sun rays hit them first, before it reached the village below. The horse nibbled the sweet grass and the chickens shared the barn. Even when the snows and winds came he knew they should count their blessings. They played hide and seek that day until their mother called them in for dinner. Rinsing their hands in the cold stream, they ran indoors still glowing from the chase.

'Now calm down children. I don't want Grandmother's best china breaking,' his mother scolded. She smiled at her son and felt proud of how hard he'd worked since her husband had died. Her little Anton. Man of the house. And her daughters, dark eyed and beautiful, would make fine wives for some lucky lads.

The sun faded, turning the trees to gold and amber, when they heard the sound of a truck revving its engine, at the bottom of the tundra. Then the masculine voices, unmistakable in their gutteral dialect, got louder.

Anton's first instinct was to protect his family, but there was no escape. The only door led straight onto the path. He opened the back window and tried to push his sisters through. Terrified they clung to their mother and cried. He closed the door behind him. Tried to put a barrier between his family and the enemy. He faced them head on.

'What do you want with us? We have nothing. Please leave us alone. We don't want any trouble.'

'Is the gypsy boy ordering us to leave?' The soldiers laughed and fired a round of rifle shot over Anton's head. He worked out the odds. There were ten of them altogether, but some had hung back, stopping to smoke a cigarette. The rest lined up outside the house, all armed. There was nothing he could do, but reason with them.

'Will you dine with me? I have rabbits if you're hungry.'

He opened the door and beckoned for his sister to go to the bedroom. Their mother stayed with Anton.

'Please gentlemen. Eat you fill. There's a pan-full of stew, fresh baked bread, current cake and soured yogurt,' she smiled nervously.

The soldiers ate the food. Then the commandant read out the orders. They had to detain Anton, his mother and three sisters for questioning, then relocation. His mother beckoned for him not to resist, calling her daughters from the bedroom. Anton stayed calm, fighting the raging exasperation inside. His Grandmother had instilled a sense of pride in him. His thoughts were going crazy on what to do for the best. When one of the soldiers grabbed his mother and roughly dragged her outside, his anger exploded. Anton threw himself at the man and started to pummel him with his fists.

He tried to put up a good fight, but they all joined in, circling round. They kept kicking him, laughing, then goading him, until he went berserk. Bit one of the soldier's leg until it bled. They lost control and smashed their rifle buts into the writhing body. The bones in his face cracked under the strain. Not once did he cry out. Not even when the blood welled in the back of his throat. His Polish pride wouldn't let him.

'Stay down,' his mother said, in the old dialect, but he couldn't. He fought until he could no longer move. And still they beat his unconscious body.

'May God protect you. My darling Anton,' his mother said, weeping quietly as they were taken to the waiting truck.

❧

Eve had never seen a man cry like this before. Not even her father at her mother's funeral. She went over to Anton and held him not saying a word - and he sobbed like a child, his whole body, racked with the remembrance of that day. His loss had been unbearable and even now, with the passage of time, his mental anguish still tormented him. She held him until he was quiet.

'I'm being all right now luff,' he said wiping his eyes. 'Why you be crying you stupid wooman?!!' he said, handing Eve a tissue. 'I never be telling no one this, not even my Maudie or Father Simon. God knowing what I be doing and he will be punishing. I finishing story? Yes!'

'Only if you want to Anton,' she replied:

'They taking mother and sisters off in truck. And leaving me for dead, but I be praying to God above to be letting me live, so I am getting revenge. I waking when it's dark, and managing to be crawling into house to be keeping alive. I not knowing how. Plenty bad pain. Maybe revenge let me living. And there being many wolves in mountains.

I lying on floor for many days, drifting in and out of unconsciousness. Not knowing how many. Then wooman from village be finding me. My mother helping her many times, so she looking after me. She fixing arm and ankle with splints and binding up tight my chest. Husband coming and taking me on cart, to house at night.'

He paused and lit a cigarette for himself and Eve, drawing the smoke deep into his lungs. She now realized why the left side of his face was sunken in at the cheek bone.

'They risking own lives but bastards not be finding me. They telling me many people being taking by soldiers, even little children luff. And many weeks I being plenty sick, spitting blood. One night, after soldiers leaving, I hearing villagers outside shouting angry, they finding shop keeper and they killing him. They burning shop down to ground and taking body up to mountains. Leaving for wolves to be eating. Nobody every be finding him - and good riddance I be saying.

Before I leaving village I going back to mother's house and cleaning it. I filling shed with logs making sure that they being warm if coming back. Putting few tins of food on shelf... I never seeing house again... Even then I feeling in my heart they being dead, luff....'

He took a gold locket hung on a faded ribbon, from inside an old Bible and showed it to her. 'Mother always wearing this...She leaving it for me to be finding. I knowing it,' he said gently. 'I getting it from in between pages about: 'turning other cheek.' He returned the locket to the Bible. The treasured item no longer hidden in The Old Testament on 'an eye for an eye.' Although the locket's outline imprinted on those pages, still showed. It now rested once more with Jesus, and forgiveness. This gesture wasn't for his own sake, but in respect for his gentle mother.

'I doing much killing after that when I joining Army, until Germans taking me P.O.W. They treating us Poles plenty bad, worse than others. Working all day, only eating water and vegetables, a few bones with bit of meat on, maybe. We catching many rats and cooking to be keeping alive. Then when War is over I coming to live in this wonderful country.'

'Did you ever see your mother and sisters again?' she asked softly.

'Never! But Father Simon he be tracing them, after I telling him about family missing. The bastards be taking them to -,' he started to cry again. 'Concentration Camp luff...Oswiecim - Auschwitz in south of Poland. They be gassing them, my beautiful mother and my innocent sisters. Russians save some poor souls in 1945...Too late for mother and sisters... And all this time luff, I never understanding... Never...'

Eve didn't know what to say. There were no words of comfort deep enough to express her sympathy, or to ease his pain. She simply said, 'I'm sorry.'

Only Sixteen

She woke up still feeling sick and not remembering much about her Sixteenth birthday party. She quickly washed and dressed realizing it was 10.a.m. The smell of Christmas Dinner cooking downstairs, made her rush to the toilet.

'Are you all right up there love?'

'Yes Mum,' she groaned, heaving into the bowl. 'Be down soon.'

When she finally managed to get into the warm kitchen a very blonde spotty youth grinned at her, in between chewing on a huge mouthful of bacon and eggs. She groaned again when she saw the food. 'Who's that?' she whispered to her mother, not remembering a thing after the third Barley Wine, except being violently sick.

'If it hadn't been for him, I don't know what would have happened to you lady!' He grinned at her. 'If he hadn't found you outside on the floor and took care of you -,' her mother said, smiling at Mitch. 'Anyone could have made off with you and we wouldn't have known anything about it.'

'Sorry Mum. Err.. Thanks...'

'Mitch,' he said.

'Here drink this!' her mother said, giving her a glass of fizzing tablets. 'You'll soon feel better. Try a bit of toast, if you can...I'm off to take these present round to June and the girls. Won't be long.'

Eve watched her mother carrying two heavy bags, one filled with presents and the other food, admiring her tenacity. The youth carried on eating his breakfast so she made some toast and sat gazing at the fire, feeling ghastly.

Rose knocked on the door of number 9 and walked in. 'It's only me Joan love,' she said, kissing the dying woman. 'Happy Christmas.'

Joan Smith smiled and beckoned her into the kitchen, she had the gas oven on to warm the room and the girls were playing with their spinning tops Joan had bought them.

'Hang on,' said Rose. 'I'll be back in a minute.'

Eve saw her mother going to the coal shed. Then filling the wheelbarrow and taking it back to no 9. Her mother's hard work and the thought of Mrs. Smith, shook her out of her own self pitying stupor.

'Want any help Mum?' she asked.

'It's all right love. Go back inside. It's freezing out here.' Rose tipped the coal into the empty shed, then chopped up some sticks.

Soon a roaring fire warmed up the bleak kitchen. 'Put the kettle on Joan. I'm parched,' Rose said, her faced flushed with exertion. She'd been up since 5.a.m. preparing the turkey and stoking up the fire to get the oven hot enough. 'Now let's open those presents girls,' she said cheerfully, but looking worriedly at their mother's tired face.

Joan opened the food bag, as the girls whooped in delight at their presents. Walkie-talkie dolls with nylon blonde hair. A chicken already cooked and stuffed, all the vegetables and a Christmas Pudding with a bottle of milk, custard powder and three crackers.

'Aren't you going to open your presents Joan love?'

As she did her beautiful haunted eyes filled with light. She held the pink knitted cardigan up against her thin body. Then put the soft gloves and scarf from Meg, to her face.

'Try the cardie on. It'll keep you nice and warm,' Rose said gently.

She helped Joan to put the vegetables on the stove, which she had already peeled in the early hours of the morning, along with her own.

'We're having a tea party for our Evie, to make up for last night. Just the family, Geoff's Mum and Jessie's lot. You and the girls are invited. I'll come and fetch you about six. If you want of course?'

'How can I ever repay you Rose?' the woman asked, barely able to stand.

'No need to, love. I know what it's like - . Anyway the more the merrier,' she laughed, kissing the younger woman.

When Rose got back to her kitchen, she saw her daughter in one chair and the lanky lad in the other. Both of them just staring into the fire, like 'two 'apenny ducks,' not talking. 'Come on buck up. Anybody would think you'd been to a funeral,' she smiled, then realized her choice of words were inappropriate. The hearse stood outside, as a bleak reminder of last night's escapades. 'Mitch love. Do you think you could park the hearse back at the Church Hall, only folks are starting to worry?'

'Certainly Mrs. Watts,' he said, jumping to his feet. He liked being fussed over and called 'love.' He'd fallen on his feet with this family, he thought - and the girl was quite nice looking, when she wasn't being sick.

Later that same Christmas night, Joan Smith put a shilling in the gas meter, turned on the oven and didn't light it. She and her girls were found by Rose the next day, peacefully asleep with their arms around each other dreaming of the happiest Christmas they'd ever had.

౮๑

After saying goodnight to Anton she walked back to the empty house. Her own distress paled into insignificance, compared to his. She knew that Maudie had been his salvation. Her love and understanding had made him a better man.

She made a warming drink and then decided to take the bull by the horns. For some time now Shirl and Mavis had tried to pair her off with many men. Those available were not exactly the pick of the bunch. Like the weird solicitor in Legal Department. Resembling Benny Hill's lecherous character. He repeated every sentence twice. Or the slick man in Administration with the three hair centre parting, who sidled up behind the girls and asked them how they were, as if he couldn't stand eye contact.

Terry Brown in Audit Department, appeared normal compared to the rest of the aging desperados. The best of a bad bunch. He was quiet and good looking, with a dry sense of humour. Five years older than herself, he owned a small farm and a big Jeep. That Christmas he'd sold free-range turkeys to most of the department. He and his mother had slaughtered, plucked and decapitated 400 turkeys that winter. He must have worked hard, she thought. Imagined his hands purple and swollen from pulling out entrails. Downy feathers mixed with gore, decorating his wellies. Bleak coldness. Aching wrists. Sore fingers and back breaking tiredness. His mother mangling necks, three a minute. If the alarm bells hadn't rung for Eve when he told her he'd never had a girlfriend, they were now about to reach 140 decibels.

Gathering up courage she decided to give him a call and wish him 'Seasons Greetings.' What was there to lose? Rejection she could take. He'd made it clear that he fancied her. Told her friends he wanted to take her out for a meal, after the divorce came through. Gave her his home phone number. Made every excuse possible to come over to her office on the pretext of work. She felt relaxed around him. He didn't seem to expect anything.

'Hello. Is that you Terry? It's Eve. Just phoning to wish you a Merry Christmas and an early Happy New Year.'

'Just a minute.'

The phone clicked down and then there was silence. After a few minutes he picked up again. She heard a door shut. 'I'm taking the call in my bedroom. How are you? Did you have a good Christmas?'

'Yes thanks. And thanks for the card...Err...I was thinking...if you want to go out for a drink some time...the "Absolute" is due in three weeks...'

'That would be grand -.' She heard a door creak open, then Terry went very quiet. A female voice in the background filtered down the phone. He covered the mouth-piece and started to reply defensively to the woman, who had obviously entered his bedroom unannounced. 'Well Jim...Thanks for letting me know about that job...Give my love to the wife and kids,' he said to Eve. Then the door closed again.

'Was that your mother?' she asked.

'Yes.'

'Doesn't she like you having female friends?'

'No.'

'Did you have to pretend I was a man?' She couldn't believe this was the motive and needed verification.

'Yes.'

Feeling a complete idiot, she abruptly ended the conversation.

Poor sod, she thought. A sign in her head flashed 'Bates Motel' as she imagined his Antony Perkins mother in a rocking chair, wearing a grey wig. But then what kind of a relationship expert was she, to pass judgment on other people's lives? She and the Soon-to-be-ex sans soul, failed miserably. She smiled at her one and only attempt at a chat up, then put on the kettle for a cup of Horlicks.

Have You Seen Her?

The Christmas Day after her Sixteenth birthday, when Mitch left the house to take the hearse back into the car park, Geoff, Stan, Johnny and Donnie were cleaning up last night's mess in the Church Hall. He waved, but didn't offer to help and started the long walk back to number 23.

'He's such a nice lad and had a terrible life. He was telling me his mother died when he was only four and that his Gran didn't want him, forcing him to work in the Funeral Parlour, when he was ten. 'Can you believe it?' her mother went on. 'I wonder what happened to Peter last night? He soon disappeared at the first sign of trouble!' she added.

'Just leave it Mum. You know we were never more that friends. And now...' she trailed off, feeling embarrassed.

'Well. It's time you had a nice boyfriend and if that's the case, then give this Mitch a chance. He seems really keen.'

'But I don't fancy him, Mum! He's like an Albino, blonde hair, blonde eyebrows, blonde eye lashes, even blonde eyes. And he got thin lips.'

'Now! Now! Evie we can't all be film stars can we?' Again Eve misinterpreted the spoken words thinking her mother also believed that she wasn't nice enough to be a Film Star, when in fact she meant the opposite.

'I suppose I could give it a try... I'm going to Vee's now Mum, to take their presents. I'll see you later.'

Eve walked through the village down to Mrs. Pound's sweet shop where Vee and Donnie rented her front room, until they'd saved enough money for a deposit on a house. She wanted to make her apologies and to give them the speech she had so carefully written.

The shop window, smeared with children's nose and finger marks, as they dreamed of a mountain of Cadbury's Roses chocolates. Full of goodies. Loose sweets bought by the scoopful and put in a triangular twist. Bulls-eyes, cinder toffee, humbugs, gob-stoppers, hammered banana toffee smashed up in the tray. Sherbert dabs, liquorice wood, barley sugar sticks and toffee apples all year round.

Inside the shop was even better, like Aladdin's Cave. Jars stacked high and filled with every kind of delight. Pear drops that made her tongue sore, fruit drops that lasted forever. Lime and lemons, and fizz bombs, aniseed balls that turned her tongue red. Sticky bonfire toffee pulled out milk teeth. Mishapes chocolates, each with an unpredictable centre. Fry's Five Boys chocolate bars. The heady fragrances from: John Horn wine gums, Newbury fruits, Winter mixtures, liquorice allsorts and Mint Imperials with a tang so strong they made her nose tingle. Here for an eternity of childlike deliberation. Buy as many as you could eat. Candy in abundance. Her Love Hearts desire. Violet chomps and Bitter lemons that gave her mouth ulcers, remedied by a dab of Bicarbonate of Soda. Sweets shining like jewels in the huge jars. Infantile paradise. No coupons required.

'Here she is the "Little Trollop",' Vee said, laughing when she saw her best friend.

'Oh! Don't say another word... I feel such a fool.'

'Let me die, just let me die!' Vee said, mocking her.

'I didn't say that... Did I?'

'You did and you threw up all over the hearse,' Vee was laughing so much it became infectious. 'Tell her Donnie, I'm not fibbing, honestly.'

Donnie kissed Eve gently on the cheek saying: 'Take no notice of her Evie. You did all right. I'd have been on the floor instantly.' Eve joined in with her friends laughter as they all opened their presents.

They toasted each other with sherry in a glass egg cups, grimaced, then put the kettle on the gas ring in the hearth.

The room had a simple leather sofa and two armchairs in the Deco style. Her friends had put their mark on the room, with photographs taken by Donnie, on every wall. Pride of place went to a wedding photo of his new wife, with the light behind her, reflecting the glints in her nut brown hair. Donnie hid all photographs of himself on their Wedding Day, in the sideboard cupboard. He couldn't stand to see himself maimed and encased in a shoulder brace.

Although he had a real talent for catching the moment, this was only his hobby. Vee filled his senses. His father now repentant, wanted them to live in the pub. He refused outright. Preferring to work in the factory alongside the men he respected from the Watts and Butterworth clans. Vee had draped streamers and paper chains everywhere and painted snow on the windows. Everything looked really cosy. Eve was pleased they'd found a haven to relax in.

His parents had visited to bring Christmas presents. Vee was pregnant and Donnie's mother so wanted to be a hand's-on Grandmother. She missed her son. She needed badly for him and his father to make-up. Donnie refused a generous cheque for a deposit on a house, but shook hands with his father. He was proud to be man of his own domain. He would provide totally and absolutely, for his young wife and future children.

The sight of Donnie's scars still shocked her. She tried not to stare too much. His forehead was worse, covered in raised livid ridges, running diagonally across just above his eyebrows and leading right up to his hairline. He had a wide scar from his lip up to his nose, but Vee said that it made him look more manly and that he was too pretty before.

Before she left Mrs. Pound's front room, she gave Vee the ointment from Mrs. Pinkerton.

'OOOO! Magic Potion!' Vee said, rubbing the pot. 'I suppose it's worth a try.'

'Vee? Will you give these presents to Peter? I can't face him after last night.' They were some silver cuff links and a book on Italian architecture.

'Honestly! You two! He's just been and said the same. He left you this.' Inside the box were the amber ear-rings. From that moment both Eve and Peter were destined to avoid each other, the one thinking the other didn't care anymore.

Eve walked back home past the factories, deeply sadden by her loss, when suddenly Mitch jumped out of the hedge. 'Want some company on the way back?'

'I thought you'd left!' she said, annoyed by his closeness.

Now Mitch mistook her indifference as playing hard to get. She suddenly became fascinating in the chase. He noticed her longs legs and titian hair and the way she bounced up and down like a pony when she walked. He was determined to win this girl over and get his feet under the table at number 23.

'Your hair is like a flock of goats!' he said, in desperation.

'What!'

'It's from The Bible. "Song of Solomon".'

'Is that a compliment then?' she said, slowing down a little.

'I think so.'

She laughed and he smiled. His milk blue eyes crinkled at the corners and he coloured up. He seemed vulnerable and she felt sorry for him.

'Your mother says I can stay for Christmas Dinner, if that's all right with you?'

'Don't see why not. A bird in the hand is worth two in the bush!' she said, remembering another of her Dad's favourite sayings. Mitch just grinned.

The mismatched pair grew to like each other. Unfortunately when Eve took two steps forward, Mitch took two steps back. Eve had been taught to go constantly onwards, regardless, so the balance of power tipped heavily in Mitch's favour - and stayed that way for twenty five years.

Every Time We Say Goodbye

31st December.

She rose early that morning still thinking about Anton. How he had suffered, but never complaining, always cheerful and generous. It was at that moment she decided to stop thinking about the future and deal with the present. She was in good health, and only the magical number of forty two. There was a slight possibility of promotion at work, if she passed her exams - and she was standing on her own two feet at last.

She took down the trimmings and threw out the Christmas and birthday cards, retrieving the one from Vee and Donnie with their new address, putting it in her hand bag for safe keeping. Vee and Donnie had been grandparents for almost eight years. She was only thirty four when her daughter gave birth. Eve decided to accept their invitation and make the long bus journey back to the village in the New Year.

The wilting Christmas tree left until the final eviction. She then cleaned the house from top to bottom - even the oven, until everything sparkled. Tuning in the radio she sat in the deck chair with a cup of tea and the last mince pie.

"Money for nothing And the chicks for free..." She smiled and found Radio 4. "Chopin's Larghetto from Serenade for Strings."

Today it was her turn to cook for Anton a typical Northern dish. Steak and kidney pie with onion gravy, bacon and cabbage mashed with butter -and Yorkshire Pudding. Followed by apple and cinnamon lattice pie with thick cream. She sang happily up to her elbows in flour, when the phone rang. 'Now what!'

It was Meg phoning to say they were back at home and that

Geoff would be there with the van early on the 2nd January. Angela had stayed sober on the way home. Meg had also given Keith a good talking to, about his roving eye. He'd promised to try again and give up this Tracey person. Eve didn't believe him but said she was pleased.

'I wish you'd come and live with us... Flats can be noisy places... You could save up for something of your own....We don't want any money. Do we Geoff?...Our Daniel wants us all to visit him for Easter and stay over. Geoff says he'll pay your fare.'

'To Canada?...I can't possibly accept Meg -.'

'Won't hear another word...There's just one thing love....Our Angela's coming too...'

'The more the merrier,' she laughed, using one of her father's sayings.

It was time for her to make her peace with Angela. Be sisters for the right reasons. Arrange outings for all three of them. She might even give Meadow Hall a try again, hoping they'd forgotten the thong incident. God was it projected on the big screen? And Angela made her laugh, when she was away from Keith. Surely they'd moved beyond sibling rivalry?

After lunch Anton went to the Polish Club and she began packing up the last few things in the kitchen cupboards. All the boxes stacked in the hall ready to be quickly moved out before the Jacksons moved in. The house echoed as she bustled around, checking cupboards and drawers. It won't always be dark at six, she thought. How she missed her Dad. She deliberately tried not to think about the last plain amber paperweight, but her curiosity got the better of her. It couldn't change things now, so what harm could it do?

She recollected trying to find Mrs. Pinkerton when it was her Nineteenth Birthday. Rose had died in April the following year of Coronary Thrombosis, just like Nan. Her mother was only 50 years old. When Eve lived at home she made sure her mother took her tablets. They were tiny pink pills and easy to swallow. She would say: 'I'm feeling all right today. I don't hold with taking tablets just for the sake of it.' Dr. Gregory confirmed that she must take them every day. Eve put the pills out for her before she went to school and when she got home, watching her mother make a face as she swallowed them.

The solemn affair of her marriage at the Registry Office

ceremony, had left her father reeling. As she walked away from the only home she'd known, on her Wedding Night, he was dumb struck. He followed her down to the end of the path holding onto her suitcase, as if he would never let go. 'Love you Dad,' she said, feeling lost.

'Me as well "Little One",' he replied and waved until they were out of sight.

Before her marriage she couldn't wait to explore new territory. Now she didn't want to leave the village. The loved/hated place where she'd spent all of her life. The cocoon valley that held them all in, and kept them there. Owned them as much as the factories and the woods around. Where every single person knew the other. Now to another county. A different culture. A different accent. A world full of strangers.

❧

If only she could go back in time and change things. Return with hindsight. Assert herself. Break the mold. It was useless to even think about what might have been. The past can't be changed. Unless a different one is invented, like Angela had done. The truth would still there, etched in granite and no amount of fantasizing would erase it.

❧

At Rose's funeral Eve reproached herself. 'If only I'd stayed. Not married and gone to the local college instead. Mum would still be alive....I would have taken care of her. Made sure she took her tablets.'

That dreadful rainy March day all the family gathered around the grave. Mitch hadn't taken the day off. He got another funeral to deal with in his home county. Angela was distraught, her legs turned to jelly. She was dumbfounded. The three sisters said their farewells, as the coffin was lowered into the wet earth. The reality agonized. They held hands, supporting each other. Something they hadn't done before. Eve felt Angela's body shaking and squeezed her hand reassuringly. Behind her Peter stood, head bowed. He'd not told anyone he would be there. At least he'd fulfilled his dream, to live in Italy, and study architecture.

167

She remembered her mother's last words to her: 'You girls must cling together, when I'm gone...And Evie, take care of Angela because she's really the babbie.' She had also said: 'You married the wrong man... It should have been Peter. He told his Mum he loved you...but when he backed off after your sixteenth birthday - . I feel responsible for pushing you into marriage at such a tender age... But, you see love, I didn't want you be alone, left on the shelf.'

Eve reassured her mother she was happy. It was a lie and her mother knew this, but simply smiled and nodded. She also remembered laughing at her mother, telling her she would outlive them all. She'd always spoken of what she would do when Stan passed away. Visit 'Vienna' and ride in a 'gombola.' Eve smiled at her mother's mix-ups. Despite the words she knew her mother's wish was to visit Italy. They shared the same dream.

Because her mother had died suddenly, she felt cheated and angry. All the things they'd planned to do and see. The life spark in her gone so quickly. None of them got to say goodbye. At first it was like a nightmare, without the frenzied waking up. There was no respite. Then gradually the pain lessened.

Peter had matured and filled out. Everyone said what a dish he'd made. He still had the same bright blue eyes and a slow smile. She studied every inch of his face. It was the same face she'd always loved. He'd grown a neat beard and his hair was longer. He wore a black woolen overcoat with his college scarf tucked inside. His soft voice made her feel safe. There were so many things unsaid. A million things they wanted to explain to each other. But the time and the place were wrong.

She wanted him to hold her. To take her back to Italy with him and bask in the warm sunshine. Away from death and away from despair. For him tell her everything would be fine. Soaked to the skin in the pouring rain, they stood close together. The tears flowed easily now among friends. Jessie was distraught. She felt as if she'd lost her right arm. Peter took hold of Eve and held her close for a minute, without saying a word. She could feel his heart beat and for a fragmentary moment, lost herself in the warmth of his body. Before she saw the signet ring on his left hand, she knew she'd lost him. Lost him for good, that night on her Sixteenth birthday. He didn't stay long, shook hands with her father and kissed her on the cheek. Nodded to the families. Then he left without looking back. The lump in her throat tightened so much, she could hardly swallow.

Stan just folded up, in shock at first, then became more and more introspective. Eve visited him as much as possible, making sure he ate properly. She couldn't bear to see him falling apart. The light had gone out of his eyes. Ever present adages, mulling in the back of his head, now dispersed into nothings. He hadn't the energy to reform them into conscious words. He still did the crossword and started to leave a few clues unresolved for her. It passed the time. She knew he could have completed it easily. He never left a crossword unfinished, but it was something to share with his daughter. They made a little game of it. She pretended not to know the clue, and he would whisper the correct word.

She visited him at weekends and he seemed a little more cheerful, especially if she stayed overnight. She felt helpless, wanted to do more for him. Meg and Angela did their best, inviting him for dinner and stop overs. He'd lost interest and became more depressed. Then one day, after she finished the crossword, he showed her a battered old shoe box, held together with a rubber band. It was filled with insurance policies. 'Just so you know where everything is,' he said.

After that he faded away. Lost without his companion. In November he died in his sleep. It said on his Death Certificate, 'Cardiac Arrest.' Jessie said to Johnny at the funeral that he'd died of a broken heart.

Eve had got him some Pacco Raban after-shave for his birthday. On reflection it was a ridiculous thing to buy. She knew he would never have the occasion, or inclination to use it. When she and Angela went to see him for the last time, in The Chapel of Rest, he looked so relaxed and peaceful in death. The anguish had gone from his face. Meg couldn't fortify herself to go with them. She and her sister sang to him. Harmonized the Everley Brothers: "Dream." Both held hands and cried, then laughed at the bizarreness of it all. When Eve patted some of the after-shave on his face, he was as cold as ice. The finality was hard to bear, but she felt closer to him through this last ludicrous gesture. One she shared with Angela.

She searched the whole of the Fairground that Christmas, but Mrs. Pinkerton was nowhere to be found. 'Why aren't you here when I really need you!' The gypsy woman had always made her feel better. Comforted her. Made her feel confidant. She felt isolated without her parents. They were the only buffer between her and life. Old Gran became more sadistic and Mitch was even worse. They despised each other, but were united in their cruelty against Eve. Both of them seemed to take delight in making her miserable.

It was Meg who was the strong one. Meg who saved her from despair. She pulled them all together as a family. Sorted out the affairs. Tied up the loose ends. Carried on the tradition of Sunday lunches, and Christmas parties. Meg the homemaker. Angela grieved more than any of them. She fell apart and it was heart breaking to see. Her radiance faded and she started to drink.

❦

She took out the small amber paperweight. Compared to the others, this simple and warm looking dome held no magic. Deep within it had flecks of red scattered like droplets of blood. The Seventh and final dome to be looked at only if she needed. She held it up to the light and peered deep into its centre. Nothing happened. Shook it, breathed on, polished it - and still nothing happened! That night she had the most terrifying nightmare.

Dancing In My Dreams

Eve sipped her usual bedtime drink, morose and alone. Her legs swollen and her spine curved. 'Years of working over a desk,' the doctor dourly informed her. She took ill-health retirement at fifty, but looked ten years older. The rented flat the final straw. It was like living in an egg box. Every sound, every bodily function magnified. Not just above, but below, at the back and either side. Other people's poverty noises, coming and going.

It was 9p.m. and she waited for the deafening music to start in the top flat. She didn't know that her flat was the first to be sold off and rented privately. The remaining flats were still occupied with Housing Benefit tenants. What had been her favourite tune, now grated on her nerves. "Everything I do I do it for you..." She knew the girl two floors above was getting ready for her gentlemen callers. She usually managed four a night. The record played over again and again, on repeat, to give her courage.

The sad youth in the middle flat, directly over her head, was an epileptic. He was having a fit - and the convulsions rattled the floor. His girl friend left their screaming baby on the landing, until he regained consciousness. Tonight, as usual, they would go out and leave the child alone, not getting back until late, start up their music to drown out the flat above them, then have clamorous sex.

Eve slept with earplugs in, they helped muffle the night sounds on the concrete steps the other side of her bedroom wall. She watched some T.V. listening through the earphones and ignored her telephone ringing out.

Draining the glass of red, she lit up a cigarette. Now she knew what Hell really was like. Feeling cold, she turned up the ancient gas fire. The landlord said he would fix it. He didn't. It gave her terrible headaches but it was better than shivering all the time. Totally exhausted she finally closed her eyes.

❧

She woke suddenly in a cold sweat in the single bed. She still clutched the amber paperweight. Replacing it in the box, she took out her favourite -the Snow-dome, then went downstairs. It was 2.a.m. New Year's Day. She made herself some hot chocolate, lit a cigarette and sat in the deck chair, feeling confused and restless.

Would it really be as bad as that, living in a flat? Meg usually gave sound advice. When the agent showed her round she thought she'd heard someone giggling in the flat above. The rent was affordable. Yet the main thing she needed right now was breathing space. Some peace and quiet. Somewhere she could paint pictures. Find her creativity again. Not have other people's misery forced into her head. It wasn't for her. She'd probably lose the deposit. Never mind. She would live with Meg instead, despite the amorous English Bull-Terrier.

The last time she'd stayed overnight with Meg, was when Geoff went to Derby to help set up another training Tool Shop. The dog immediately took a shine to her. He was all white with a black patch over one eye, like Bulls-eye in "Oliver Twist." A huge fat pot-bellied pig. During the night he managed to open the bedroom door, then snuffled and grunted under the duvet. Holding her feet between his paws, he growled if she moved. She stayed that way all night, with 'Dinosaur Head' snoring and farting, until Meg brought her a cup of tea the next morning.

She would go to Florence and find Peter. Finance the holiday with a loan. Draw out the few hundred pounds in her Building Society Account. She had to try to speak to him. Clear the air. How hard could it be to find an English architect in Florence? He would be in the 'phone book. She desperately needed a holiday, a change from the daily grind.

Settling back in the deck chair, she gave the dome a good shake. It was so beautiful with the white rose in the centre and the snow, gently falling. Her eyes felt heavy and swollen so she placed the cool glass against them and dreamed of finding Peter and Italy.

❧

Vee and Donnie took them to the airport in their clapped out Mini car. The exhaust steamed out in the cold night air and they chugged along for hours, until they finally arrived at their destination. Suitcases jammed packed with paints and sketch pads. None of them had ever seen a plane before, except at the cinema. The hustle and bustle of the departure lounge was something new to them. So many people talking at the same time. Not one of them knowing the other. A whole building full of people with downcast eyes. Not looking at each other, showing no interest in what the other did. In the village everyone stared, regardless of the circumstances. If someone fell on their backside here, they'd most likely trip over them, before they noticed. Vee felt nervous and exhilarated at the same time, wishing she could go with them. She'd left her baby daughter Beth, with her mother.

Vee had hoped her friend would become a mother soon, so they could share things again. Now she realized this was a false hope, for a while at least. Her friend had bigger things to achieve. 'Can we get a cup of tea here?' she asked. 'I'm gagging.'

As Donnie and Peter went for the beverages, Vee read out the order of flights on the notice board.

'I'll miss you Evie Watts,' she said.

'Me too Vee. I'll write every week...You and Donnie will come and visit in the summer? We'll show you the sights. Your Mum said she'll look after Beth for two weeks.'

'This is for you,' Vee said grinning. She handed Eve a wrapped gift. Inside was a five year diary and a box of condoms. 'The diary's for when you get a break from the rampant sex,' she laughed. 'I want to know every minute of what's happening. Every sight and sound you experience, so as I can feel them too...Paint me a picture of "Vienna" and a "gombola" to remind me of your Mam.'

The two young women hugged each other feeling tearful. There hadn't been a day since their first encounter in Yarmouth, when they didn't share a secret, or laugh at their parents' dilemmas. Now they would be apart for two years.

'Wipe your eyes Evie. Make yourself look beautiful. It's that James Dean look-alike bloke and lanky Peetrill heading our way. Do you think we might pull?'

'What's going on?' Donnie said, smiling at his wife.

'Why? Were your ears burning love?' Vee said. 'Look at this Evie, tea in a plastic cup. Whatever next...What's that supposed to be, when it's at home,' she said, pointing to a Danish pastry. 'It looks like a worm fossil...Didn't they have any Eccles cakes?' Eve thought fondly, how much Vee sounded like her mother. Jessie who had made everybody laugh with her antics. Her door always open to children. She even let Eve and Vee play in the front room, among the china birds. Vee's father just smiled all the time.

Eve thought back on the first time she'd had called for Vee on her way to school. There was pandemonium in the house. Everyone fighting for toast. Ted dipping in Vivian's boiled egg, and Freddie taking a huge bite out of Vee's bacon sandwich.

'Do you want a sandwich love?' Jessie asked her.

'No thanks Mrs. Sharp. I've had porridge.'

'Here,' she said, shoving a door-step sized bacon sandwich into her hand. 'This'll grease your bones lass...Get some "Daddies"' sauce on it.'

Eve learned that Jessie refused to take 'no' for an answer. Also she wouldn't tolerate waste of food. Every last crumb must vanish, especially at tea time. It was chips with everything and Eve loved chips. They never got them at school dinners. Best of all were the chip fights the Butterworth children had, as their mother bustled around in the noisy kitchen. Ted and Freddie were always the instigators. The girls learned to catch the chips as they were thrown. Then eat the spoils before the boys could claim them back. Jessie pretended to be annoyed with her rowdy bunch, but she never stopped them having fun.

"The Four Musketeers" in the airport lounge, drank their tea in silence, feeling as if something important was disappearing.

'The 2015 flight to Pisa is now ready for boarding,' a nasal voice announced.

They did a group hug, knowing childhood was over. That it only existed in their memories from now on. None of them moved, trying to hold onto the moment as long as possible. The crowd blurred into silence. Emotions stirred. Memories flooded back. Things changed.

Moved on to another phase. Then Eve and Peter went through the barrier control, hand in hand, turning for a final wave.

'Italy here we come!' Peter said, as they disappeared through the narrow corridor, punching the air.

Eve missed her friends already. No matter where life took her from now on, she would always remember the girl in the knitted swim suit. Vee, who brought laughter into her little life. The quiet boy with the ridiculously large car, showing them life from a different perspective. And Charlie running after her calling out: 'Wait for me Beebie.'

"Spots in time," she thought, understanding Wordsworth.

As Eve fastened her safety belt, she became extremely nervous, until Peter entwined her finger with his own, and said everything would be all right. Planes are safe as houses he told her. Flying above the clouds was magical. Even more magical was peering through the white fleece and looking down at nothing but sea. They talked non stop through the flight meal, about the house that would be their base for the next two years. Wondering what the Italian family of artist and musicians, would be like.

Eve slept peacefully, until a light shining overhead woke her. Someone wanted to read, she thought. She was cold and reached out for a blanket, Peter breathed evenly and relaxed. Then she tried to adjust her seat into recline. The deck-chair collapsed under her weight. 'Bugger!'

⁊

Come hell or high-water she was determined finish the dream. Get it off her chest. Make an end to false hopes. Find the end of the rainbow. Burst the bubble. Take a reality test. The Sixties have a lot to answer for. Coulda! Shouda! Woulda! Think and make it happen. Man is the measure of all things. All things come to he who waits. It suddenly hit her. Her father had used these comforters like a shield, to protect her from the grosser picture of life. Shit! Speaking in parables next, she thought.

⁊

The light, brilliant and so different to that she'd known, made her want to set out an eisel straight away. The air intoxicating, as they sped away from the airport towards Florence. Rows of cypress and olive trees hugging the mountain, all the way up to Vaglia and the Bochelli family.

'Peter. It's just like the book. Bright and glorious.'

'Better,' he said, not wanting to miss a moment. Trying to take everything in at once, like a kid in Hamley's.

'What shall we see first?' she asked, knowing his answer.

'What do you think?... "The Uffizi" of course, then the statue of David.'

'I can't believe were actually here.'

'Me neither,' he said, pinching her and laughing. 'There you are. It's real.'

'Do you think the Bochelli family will like us? They seemed really nice in their letters,' she asked.

'Beatrice said you could share her room. Sandro has an old Fiat to drive us around in to see the sights...Or we could hire a scooter... We'll be fine,' he said, putting his arm round her.

'I'm so nervous. It's worse than pre-exams.'

'Can't be. Nothings worse than running to the loo with the trots, five minutes before the clock chimes on the start hour.

They both chuckled.

Don't stop. Go on. Kiss me properly, before I wake. Please. Just once. Something to remember. She screwed her eyes up and forced herself to finish off the dream. It disappeared in a Beam me up Scottie moment. Dissolved into thin air. Bugger!

What a sad cow I've turned into, she thought, feeling exhausted. Living to dream. Filled with 'airy nothings.' Time and tide wait for no man. Would she ever get these bloody sayings out of her head? She doubted it. Just as Hellfire and Damnation were impregnated there, so would her father's choice-phrases stay with her for the rest of her life. Along with: Power to the People, Singing in the Rain, Least said soon is mended, May the force be with you, Swear not by the moon, Don't titter missus, Windmills of your mind, Tis a far far better thing I do, I can't get no satisfaction, Absence makes the heart grow fonder, Viennese Gombolas, Lassie come Home, Songs of Praise, Up the Owls, Where there's muck there's brass, Follow the yellow brick road, A nod's as good as a wink to a blind man, A play what I wrote, Say goodnight Gracie, All Cows Eat Grass, Elvis has left the building, Hancock's Half Hour, One giant leap for Mankind, That's all folks, Love thy Neighbour, and A single man in possession of a good fortune must be in want of a wife. It was 3.00a.m. as she wearily climbed the stairs and settled into the tiny bed for the last time in the marital home, feeling strangely relaxed and comforted by her Christmas holiday reverie.

You Are Always On My Mind

A fine mist hung over the trees obscuring the visibility of the two men walking towards the rambling old house. The younger man was play fighting with two Springer spaniels and laughing, while the older man tried to push them away with his walking stick. They both talked loudly shouting at the dogs, their breath steaming out in front of them. Walking up the drive their boots crunched on the gravel and set the dogs barking even more, as the house gradually appeared in front of them.

There was a holly wreath covered in red berries fixed on the enormous paneled door and through the hall window the fairy lights shone on a ceiling-high Christmas tree. A warm glow reflected through the kitchen window and the log firelight flickering on the walls was so inviting to the men - and the thought of the mulled ale waiting for them when they got inside.

'WAKING UP LUFF! DOGS EATING TURKEY HEAD!'

'Now what!'

Eve stretched and yawned, then reached for her dressing gown, as Anton banged on the bedroom window, disturbing her dream of a desolate old age, sick and alone. She opened the curtains and wondered why, today of all days, he was cleaning windows in the freezing cold, but nothing would stop him once he'd made up his mind.

'Happy New Year luff!' he chuckled. 'Be quicking everybody else is being up for ages.'

She showered, brushed her hair, then slipped on a pair of slacks and a polo neck, smiling at the photographs on the dressing table. She was so proud of Jenny and Thomas even though they were making their usual racket outside. Her daughter, who never wanted to have intimate discussions. She was fiercely independent and quick-witted.

Didn't suffer fools. Needed her parents to be comfortable oldies, not weekend joggers. Didn't like the male students fancying her mother. She saved her inner-most thoughts to share with her friends at college. Three generations of women had moved full circle in their views on life.

But Thomas, laughing, happy Thomas, confided in her. He was always affectionate and mischievous. He couldn't keep a secret and often told her of his innermost desires.

'Come on Evie love. Your breakfast's getting cold.'

'Mum?'

'Now then "Greer Garson", get yourself down here quick.' She ran down the stairs, along the hall and into the kitchen. 'Early to bed, early to rise...!' her father said, laughing. 'What's wrong love you look as if you've seen a ghost?'

'I had this awful dream...that you and Mum were dead and I was married to an embalmer...'

'Too many bloody glasses of vino last night Evie,' Angela said, nodding to Ken.

'And you were married to that Fairground lad. Do you remember, the one with the black curls.'

'Could have had him, you know,' she said to Ken. 'If it hadn't been for that bloody gypsy's warning.'

'You still married a "K". Didn't you Angela!' Meg said, laughing.

'He's the right "K" though. Not the wrong "K",' said Rose. 'Aren't you Ken?' Rose had an affinity with Ken. They understood each other. Both were born under the same star sign: Libra. Ken smiled in his easy going way.

'What else did you dream Evie?' her mother asked, handing her a cup of tea. Eve took in every inch of her mother's dear face, as if she'd not seen it for years.

'I didn't go to college and lived in a Funeral Parlour with the embalmer and his evil Old Gran, instead,' she went on.

'What's this about an embalmer,' her husband said, kissing her neck and nuzzling his cold nose under her ear.

'Darling!' she said, throwing her arms round him.

'Steady on. I've only been gone an hour,' he laughed.

'Did you rescue the turkey from the dogs then lad?' Stan said.

'Just about, although the neck and head aren't much good for gravy Ma!'

The welcoming sight of Anton coming in from the cold brought Eve back to the present. 'I cleaning all windows luff, bringing Good Luck for New Year.' She hugged him tightly. 'Be slowing down love. I not be going away,' he chuckled.

'It's a wopper,' Vee said. 'Must have taken some carrying, especially with two mad dogs trying to worry it.'

'Vee!' Eve said, hugging her best friend. 'I dreamed that we lost touch and I never saw you again. Where's Donnie?'

'It's getting more like the bloody "Wizard of Oz" by the minute,' Jessie exclaimed.

'She'll be looking for the chuffing ruby slippers next,' Angela said, roiling her eyes.

'Now. Now. Angela. Less of that sort of language, if you please,' her mother said.

Donnie was looking intensely at the paintings set out and numbered, on the first landing above the winding staircase. Eve noticed that his scars were now faint white lines, as he came down to kiss her. 'Happy New Year Evie. I love the paintings of the gondolas.'

'For you and Vee, if you want it?'

'Out of our price range, "Mrs. Money Bags",' Vee said, teasing her friend.

'It's a gift, for all the years of happiness you've given me,' she said.

'Bloody Hell Evie. You're getting sentimental in your old age!' Angela said. 'Can we have the one of Florence?'

'You being no bloody Spring chicken yourself,' Anton said, echoing one of Stan's sayings, as he went upstairs to change.

'Not that one sis,' Eve smiled at her sister. Angela's barbed comments didn't hurt anymore, not since she'd entered the mysterious world of womanhood, only to find that it was no different to the hopeful world of childhood. 'I've done a special one for you. It's drying in the studio.'

Angela and Ken went into the room adjoining the kitchen and saw the portrait. The girl's fresh face, lifted up to the light and glowing with vitality, her hair shining like a halo. And she wore a tight red top and a candy pink skirt with swirling petticoats, enfolding her young body like the petals on a flower.

'You look beautiful,' Ken whispered in her ear.

'I had my moments,' she said, trying to pose in the same way as the portrait.

Jenny and Thomas were outside playing with Starsky and Hutch, the dogs, and pushing into each other, skidding on the icy lawn. Then the slim girl with strawberry blonde hair and rosy cheeks, laughed helplessly, while the boy with vivid blue eyes and auburn curls spun her round until she was dizzy.

Nan Hill joined in, throwing a frisby for the tireless spaniels, while Granddad pushed them away with his stick when they came bounding back. He decided it was time to go inside for that long awaited warming drink, singing out: 'Come on Eileen...'

Eve finished her toast, wondering if she was still dreaming and hoping she would never wake up. A fat black mog squeezed in through the cat-flap.

'Hello old Brutus,' Stan said, affectionately. The crazy feral cat got his name because one of his ears was missing. He terrified the dogs and ruled the roost. The foul feline growled softly and curled up into a ball on the hearth rug.

Jenny and Thomas came crashing into the kitchen. 'We've got hot-aches Granddad Stan,' Thomas groaned.

He took out two tea cloths from the cupboard and warmed them in front of the fire. Then wrapped his grandchildren's hand. Smiling his contented smile.

'It always works,' laughed Jenny.

'For goodness sake take off your wellies,' Rose said to them, grabbing the mop and bucket from the utility room.

Following dinner Eve sat on the sofa, resting her head on her husband's shoulder.

'I wonder what I've done to deserve you?' she asked.

'Well?... You didn't complain when I stepped on your feet during our first dance,' he said, smiling. 'And when you gave me my first real kiss I buckled at the knees.'

'That's it! The embalmer!' she said.

'You're not still banging on about that?' said Angela, snuggling up to Ken. They were trying to watch "It's a Wonderful Life," on the T.V.

'Do you remember, Peter? When Billie Biddle phoned from "The Blue Bell" on the pass, and said they couldn't make it. Some 'daft fart' driving a hearse had skidded on the ice trying to overtake them. They all ended up the ditch and it nearly killed them.'

'Yes. How could I forget the merry tunes of Billie. Had a better time without them though.'

'Aye! It's all coming back to me now,' said Johnny. 'And the 'daft fart' was going to buy them drinks all night, or else they'd kill him.'

'That's who was in my nightmare.'

'I remember lass. It snowed like Billyho!' said Jessie.

'Shhh!' said Angela.

Jessie came over to the other sofa, her curly brown hair now white as snow, and whispered. 'Can you remember? Johnny pushing the old wind-up gramophone in the wheelbarrow. And us slipping and sliding with our best frocks under our macs, trying not to drop the bloody records.'

'And we had to drag the food on the boys' sledges, through the snow. I don't know how we kept those trifles in one piece,' Rose said.

'Geoff took some in the sidecar on his bike. And our Angela stacked up the old Ford Pop with sandwiches and party hats,' Meg laughed.

'And Evie's and Peter's speeches... They were both so nervous at first, until Jessie started heckling them,' Stan said.

'Funny how things turn out,' Geoff added.

Later that afternoon after dinner, Eve asked her husband if the boxes had been collected. He'd sorted out the attic over a week ago and put the stuff at the bottom of the drive.

'The woman from the W.V.S. came. A bit odd looking to say the least. Not at all what I was expecting, you know: felt hat, belted coat and brogues... This one was really weird.'

'Like a pantomime dame?'

'Yes! How do you know? You were still asleep.'

'Oh! Everyone knows her lad. It's Mrs. Pinkerton!' Rose said.

'She had the funniest hair I ever seen and eyebrows up into her forehead. Anyway she ignored all the boxes except that little gold cardboard one you put out, with the glass domes in.'

'Did she say anything?'

'Something about you didn't need them anymore and someone else would be glad of them.'

Eve smiled. 'Is that all? No gypsy warning?'

'No. Nothing else.'

She wrapped up warmly and told everyone she wouldn't be away for long. She walked down the drive to the gates to see if the rest of the junk had gone. Her breath steamed out in front of her. A woman in a felt hat and belted coat was loading it into the back of a van. Her brogues shone like mirrors.

'Thanks Mrs. Hill. They'll go to a good cause. 'Happy New Year',' she said, climbing into the van.

'Same to you. See you after the holidays... Drive carefully Mrs. Sullivan it's turning into a pea-souper,' Eve said, waving until the van was engulfed by the mist.

She was just about to return to the house when a familiar voice came through the mist. 'Hello! Flame-haired child. Long time no see!'

'Mrs. Pinkerton!...' she said, startled by the sudden appearance of a figure in an emerald green velvet cape and yellow wellies. 'Will you come back to the house for a warm and something to eat?'

'No child, my purpose is done! It's a pity you didn't spot the rare hidden butterfly paperweight sooner. It's worth an absolute fortune and would take you to Italy many times over.'

'Am I dreaming? And if not, why me? Mrs. Pinkerton? What have I done to deserve this heaven?'

'What is the difference between dreams and reality anyway? The five sense are very limited...Imagination is everything dear girl... Hopes and dreams help us live on -.'

'Please let me continue to dream. For a little while longer, at least. This is everything I've ever wanted.'

'Nothing is perfect, except heaven itself - and the angels within,' the gypsy said. 'In my line of work I try to help many people...The world is a harsh place to live in for those deprived of understanding. Even so, not many of them listen to a gypsy's warning...Look what happened to Troy!' she sighed.

Eve thought she couldn't possibly be referring to Homer's "Iliad," then remembered Troy Donague. 'I used to have a crush on him.'

'Never mind!' She sighed even deeper. 'Do you have a cigarette?'

Eve took a packet of Benson and Hedges out of her pocket and handed them to the gypsy. 'I'm giving up for the New Year,' she said, smiling. 'I'll share a last cigarette with you Mrs. Pinkerton.'

'You were one of the few who always came to me and listened. There are many paths to take in life. Some choose the right ones, others don't have a choice... But now my time is finished here!' she said, blowing out a stream of smoke into the cold air and putting the cigarette packet inside her cape.

Eve crossed the gypsy's palm with silver - a five pence piece she'd found in the corner of her pocket.

'Can I ask you something?... Why didn't you help Joan Smith instead - or Anton's family?'

'Darling Anton...' she sighed... 'What can a mere gypsy do? I only read the signs...Such greater burdens are left in the hands of God!' she said wearily.

'If I'm dreaming please don't pinch me. I don't ever want to wake up from all this,' Eve said, holding on to the moment.

'We all have to face our own reality child,' she answered.

Eve kissed the woman on her pink and powdered cheek, smelling the heady perfume. "Devon Violets!" Mrs. Pinkerton began sneezing wildy.

'Do you have a cat?' she asked, still spluttering.

'Yes. Old Brutus...Why?'

'Hate them... I am allergic to the feline monsters.'

'Do you think it's going to snow for New Year's Day?' Eve asked, changing the subject. The gypsy wiped her running eyes and turned to walk away. She'd never seen Mrs. Pinkerton standing before and suddenly realized what an imposing figure she presented. Six feet tall at least, in her wellies.

'What you expect for one shilling - a miracle?' she said, turning and winking at her. Then in a blur of green and yellow, she disappeared into the mist.

If this was another illusion and she was about to wake up, she wouldn't waste any more time, or energy, on negative thoughts. "The path of life can only go forward," she thought. Echoing her father's well-worn wisdom. Eve knew from now on, she'd do what she wanted most, not what was expected of her.

The sound of her boots on the gravel path. A biting coldness made her shiver. Unable to see her hand in front of her face. The smell of wood smoke sullying the air. Silence among the fir trees. The house with glowing lights no longer visible. Birds no longer clucking in the shadows. Dogs stopped barking. Christmas passed. New Year's Day finished. The smell of cooking disappeared as the greyness enfolded her. Only the sound of her boots on the gravel path guided her back - a reassuring noise in the silent fog. Then the hammering started, quietly at first, becoming louder as she reached the end of the path.

'WAKING UP LUFF! BROTHER-IN-LAW FETCHING VAN OUTSIDE! MAD CAT JUMPING ON SISTER'S PIG-DOG'S BACK! BE QUICKING TO COMING DOWN.'

ↂ

About the Author

The author has two other published novels: My Wicked Aunt Leonora and Wrong Time: Right Face. Her favourite hobby of writing has become a full time job. She has also written many children's stories and has had some success in poetry competitions.

Lightning Source UK Ltd.
Milton Keynes UK
UKOW05f0618130813

215249UK00002B/145/P

9 781481 788960